THE GHOST HUNTER CHRONICLES

ASHES TO ASHES

BOOK 2

T.R. ALLARDICE

When Alexa Dawn was thirteen-years-old, her parents were murdered by a ghost that she contacted through a game board.

It let her live.

That was its first mistake.

Now Alexa is twenty and it's back. This time it's determined to take out her clients and friends.

Coming back was its second mistake.

There won't be a third.

Chapter One

Kissing should be the last thing you think about on the way to a crime scene, but for some reason, I could think of little else. Detective Adam Grayson and I hadn't discussed what had taken place last night. What was there to say? We'd come close to bopping like bunnies, but I'd backed out at the last minute. I'm good at that. Just ask anyone.

Okay, I admit I was scared. Somehow, he'd gotten under my skin and I knew that if I had stuck around there would have been more than sex happening. Adam didn't seem like a one-night-stand kind of guy. He seemed like the kind of guy you could count on to be there in the morning. The kind of guy who'd want a relationship afterwards.

I didn't do relationships. Relationships made you vulnerable. Left you open to being hurt. I couldn't survive that kind of pain again. The fact that I'd come close to breaking my dating rules for him spoke volumes.

The sun caressed the treetops, leaving light freckles on the gray sidewalks. The cars parked in the driveways blurred before my eyes, their colors a swirl of mismatched paint as we passed several miniature ranch homes before reaching our destination.

A white van with fat blue letters scrolled on the side of it sat parked beneath a bushy-headed oak with thick-knotted branches. I caught the word cleanup, before spotting something far more disturbing—Stephen Reynolds's car rolling to a stop behind the van. We swung into the Hawkins' driveway.

"What is he doing here?" I said more to myself than to Adam. I craned my neck to see, and watched Stephen step out of the Nova.

"Isn't that your boyfriend, Alexa?" Adam asked.

"Ex, remember? But you already knew that or you wouldn't have tried to seduce me last night." With one look, I dared Adam to refute my claim.

His lips twitched. "How do you know that I'm so noble? I wasn't exactly following police procedure last night."

I smirked. "Call it a hunch."

"Smart girl." His smile slowly faded and his expression turned serious. "I want to thank you for putting a stop to last night. I shouldn't have—it was wrong. Thanks."

Not exactly what I'd hoped to hear from him, but I'd take what I could get. "You're welcome."

He reached for my hand. "You were right to put the brakes on. It's better if we wait until the cases are closed."

I nodded in agreement because I couldn't think of what else to say. It was the right thing to do. Logically, I knew that, but logic wouldn't keep me warm at night.

He glanced past me out the window. "I suppose we should go find out what he wants, since the scene is still off limits. The cleanup crew won't be allowed in until tomorrow."

"How do you know?"

His eyes twinkled. "I haven't signed the sheet, giving them permission to enter."

"Good reason."

He laughed. "I thought so."

I jumped out of Adam's car the second it rolled to a stop.

Stephen stood on the other side of the crime scene tape. "What are you doing here?" I asked.

"Good to see you too, Lex," he said, before catching a glimpse of Adam. Stephen's smile turned brittle. "What is he doing here? You should be tired of him by now."

"Cop, remember?"

Stephen shrugged as if that bit of information was irrelevant.

My hands rested on my hips. "Now I'm going to ask you again. What are you doing here?"

Stephen glanced over his shoulder toward the cleanup van and nodded at the two men inside. One read a *Sports Illustrated*, while the other chatted on a cell-phone and munched potato chips. Neither looked bright enough to open the van doors without help.

"Friends of yours?" I asked.

He pointed to the guy scarfing down chips. "The one on the left is my buddy, Brad. He's going to let me in to investigate, once they finish cleaning up."

I grabbed Stephen by the forearms. "Listen, you have to let this one go. This isn't like a normal investigation. People are dying."

He pulled out of my grip. "Of course they are. That's why I followed you."

"This isn't a joke, Stephen."

"I know." He tugged at his sleeves. "I told Finn that you have been holding out on us. The murders have been all over the news. *You've* been all over the news. I knew there was no way you'd be anywhere near these crime scenes if there wasn't a major haunt taking place. Unless, you've suddenly gone psycho and killed all those people." He eyed me, trying the possibility on for size. "Nah." Stephen laughed. "You may be a supreme bitch, but you aren't a murderer."

"Thanks." I grimaced. "I appreciate the vote of confidence."

He grinned, a lopsided flash of teeth that at one point in

time I would've found cute. Not anymore. I recognized it for what it was, a seductively casual way to manipulate. Stephen wore black pants and a loose gray shirt that opened at the collar, exposing his throat and pale skin. His blond hair blew into his eyes and he swept it aside in a practiced move that used to set my heart aflutter.

I was shocked once more to realize that I felt nothing but sorry for him. Not even a hint of the emotion that had bonded us so many months ago remained. Pity. At one time, he'd been a really good friend. But now, that was gone, too. Even so, I couldn't just let him walk into a dangerous situation without warning him.

"You need to listen to me and listen carefully. This has nothing to do with us," I said.

He scowled. "By us, do you mean you and I or are you referring to you and the cop?"

"I don't have time for your jealous nonsense. I have to go into that house now. Do yourself a favor and stay the hell away from the Changs' and the Hawkins's homes until the police wrap up their investigation."

Stephen's eyes narrowed and I saw a newfound determination in his expression that frightened me. "I never realized you were so territorial about your investigations. I'll have to let Finn know," he said. "No wonder the team never found anything on the nights that you were with us. You probably rigged our equipment or tampered with the evidence."

I rolled my eyes. "There was no evidence, Sherlock."

"You expect me to take your word for it after all the lies you've told us?"

I showed remarkable restraint as I shoved my hands into my pockets to keep from punching him in the face. "Are you even listening to yourself?"

He stepped closer. "Truth hurts. Doesn't it?"

My voice softened, pleading for him to believe me. "I mean it, Stephen. I'm not kidding when I say that these locations are dangerous. I've never encountered anything like these haunts," I said. "I'm scared. And you know if I'm scared, they are bad."

Stephen stared at me for so long I almost thought that he hadn't heard me. I had no idea what he was looking for in my expression, but he must have found it. Reluctantly, he nodded. "Fine. If it means that much to you, I will investigate somewhere else."

"Thank you." I brushed his arm.

His quick surrender made me nervous. Stephen never gave up that easy. I once saw him argue with Finn until three in the morning over the font setting in the Paranormal Friends Society's newsletter. Not because it mattered, but because he didn't want to lose the argument. In the end, Finn gave up and let Stephen have his way.

"This is important," I reiterated.

"I said I'd investigate elsewhere and I will. I hope you know that I wouldn't do this for just anyone," he said.

I watched his expression, trying to discern if he was lying to me. Unfortunately, I couldn't tell, so I let it slide. "I appreciate it," I said reluctantly.

He stepped closer, crowding my personal space. "Do you mean that, Lex? Are you really grateful that I'm going to stay out of your way?"

Suspicion tickled my gut. "Yes," I answered cautiously.

He gave me a knowing smile. "I can think of a few ways that you can prove it." He reached out to touch me.

I sidestepped to avoid his hand. "Not happening," I said.

Stephen suddenly straightened. "Have it your way." He glanced over my head and his body tensed. "I think your new boyfriend wants you."

My retort was immediate. "He's not my—"

Stephen held up his hand. "Save it, Lex. I've seen how he looks at you. If you aren't sleeping with him already, you will be soon."

I didn't answer him. What could I say? Well, yes. You're

right. We almost had sex last night. I didn't think that Stephen would appreciate that level of honesty. Besides, I really wanted him to stay away from this house and the others. That wouldn't happen, if I pricked his ego.

"Got to go." I walked over to Adam, who'd been casually watching us.

When I got close, he put his arm around me and pulled me against his chest. Shocked by the public display of affection, I looked into his face, but he wasn't staring at me. Adam's gaze was locked on the sidewalk, where I'd left Stephen.

Men. I rolled my eyes, then pulled out of his grasp.

"Really? Try beating your chest next time. I hear it works well for primates." I shook my head and left them to their silent face-off.

* * * * *

Finding out anything else about the Hawkins family murders had been wishful thinking on our part. Crime scene investigators had bagged and tagged anything of relevance, leaving only empty spaces behind. Blood still stained the walls, floor, and ceiling in the kitchen, and would continue to do so until the cleaning crew gained access. Someone had removed the chalkboard, for which I was grateful. I didn't want to see the message again.

I hadn't spotted the Shade or Huli Jing. Although I wasn't altogether convinced that I'd seen her here in the first place.

An Amber alert had been issued for Ryan Hawkins. No vehicle was mentioned in the broadcasts, only a detailed description of Ryan. As much as I wanted to believe that he'd somehow escaped the brutal attack, I knew that was unlikely.

This mess made the Manson family's work look amateurish. No human had created this devastation. I tried not to think of the seven kinds of hell Ryan must've gone through if it killed him last and took his body with it. I didn't even want to consider the possibility it was keeping him breathing, like some kind of living trophy.

Why would it leave me alone and take Ryan? What made me so special? I shivered. Therapists called what I felt survivor's guilt. It happened sometimes when a person survived something horrific, but the people around them died. The only thing I agreed with them on was the guilt part. I had it in spades.

"You about ready to go?" Adam asked.

"Yes." I looked around the room one last time. "There's nothing left here."

Adam walked out of the kitchen and I trailed behind.

I stepped into the living room, seeing it again as it used to be. Mr. and Mrs. Hawkins would've been seated on the couch, their backs resting against the blue afghan. Mr. Hawkins would've been reading the paper, while Mrs. Hawkins crocheted. The Ryan that I knew would've been on the floor, playing with his *Thomas the Train*.

A lump formed in my throat and I looked away. "Do you think there's a chance he's still alive?" I asked.

There was a moment of silence, then a quiet sigh. "No. Even if he survived his parents' attack, I doubt the killer would let him live past a few hours of amusement."

I winced. I couldn't help it. I pictured Ryan tied to a string like Mr. Wiggle's toy.

"I'm going to take a quick look around the backyard. Do you want to wait here or come with me?" Adam asked.

The house was quiet. A few minutes alone would give me time to reflect and come up with a strategy. "I think I'll stay here."

Adam tugged my arm, pulling me around to face him. "You sure?" He stroked my arm soothingly.

I nodded. "Go on. The sooner you get that done, the sooner we can get out of here."

He squeezed my shoulder as he passed. In his absence the silence I'd found comfort in moments ago turned sinister. I took a step toward the front door and saw a dark head pop up like a shark's fin on the other side of the couch.

I did a double take. The dark head was still there, cruising silently along the back of the couch, positioning itself between me and escape. My senses went on high alert. I tried to breathe, but my chest constricted.

Huli Jing stepped out from behind the furniture and smiled. My three-foot-tall nightmare had returned, looking fresh-faced and innocent as she stood near the front door. The frightening mask no longer fooled me.

Her dark eyes were back, but I knew the flames weren't far behind. The hair on my neck and arms rose with the static charge she produced. I reached into my pocket and felt emptiness, forgetting for a moment that I didn't have any of my equipment with me. I took a side step, judging the distance to the door. I didn't dare take my eyes off her. There was no way I'd make it before she reached me.

The burn on my shoulder began to throb and ache. I gripped it, breathing through the pain. "What are you doing here?"

She cocked her head and scowled, but didn't answer. I don't know why I expected her to. She hadn't the last time we met. Did she like to come back to the scene of her crimes? Admire her handiwork? Or just to taunt me? I thought about the message on the board in the kitchen. Was she working with the Shade that killed my family? Were they some kind of murderous tag team?

That was a horrifying thought.

I began a slow retreat toward the kitchen where the back door was located. None of this made any sense. I was missing something and I had no idea what. Huli mirrored my steps, slowly closing the distance between us.

I chanced a glance over my shoulder to see how far away the kitchen was and if I could make it before she reached me. My eyes strayed to the picture window on the far wall. I'd go through the glass if I had to. The temperature began to drop.

My body quaked, but it had nothing to do with the cold.

"What did you do with the boy?" I asked. "Where is Ryan?"

That question seemed to give her pause. A small frown dimpled her brow. Her eyes darkened, then flickered. Was that concern or surprise? I couldn't be sure. Did she even feel emotions? I'd seen her cry, but that had been an act. In the next instant, I didn't care because pressure crushed down upon me.

"You bitch," I shouted as I grabbed my head and doubled over in pain. "You fucking demon bitch. I'm going to kill you."

"You shouldn't be here," she said, using the voice of a child. "They're gone. There's nothing left for you to consume."

I folded in on myself in an attempt to escape the pain. "They who?" What did she mean by consume?

Before she could answer, the door flew open behind me. "Alexa, are you all right?" Adam rushed forward.

With great effort, I twisted to one side. "Adam, run! Get out of here before she gets you."

He stopped abruptly with an odd expression upon his face. "Before who gets me?"

I pointed at Huli. "Her."

She grinned. Her amused macabre expression sent shivers along my spine. "He can't see me."

Adam glanced around frantically. "I don't see anyone."

My hand shook as I pointed to where she'd stood. "She's right there." Oh God, was I the only one who could see her?

"The room is empty," he said. "We're the only ones here, Lex."

Huli grinned at me one last time, then disappeared.

A moment later, the temperature returned to normal. I released my head and straightened, the pain a fading memory. Cautiously, I approached the couch and looked behind it. Nothing. "Where did she go?" My search turned frantic as I scoured the living room.

"You want to tell me what's going on?" he asked. Adam moved closer and gripped my shoulders to stop me. "There's nothing here, Alexa."

I growled in frustration "I know that, Adam. I can see."

His hands slid up to my shoulders, where he began to massage the tension knotting my neck. "Then why did you tell me to run?"

"Because I thought...I thought... " I rubbed my temples. "Forget it. I think I'm just tired. My mind is playing tricks on me. I'm seeing things that aren't there."

"Like Huli Jing?"

I tried to smile, but it came out like more of a grimace. "Yeah, like her."

"Wait here." Adam searched the whole house. I wasn't sure if he'd done it for my benefit or for his. When he returned he said, "The house is definitely empty."

Why hadn't Adam been able to see her when he came into the room? It wasn't like she was hiding. "It was probably just my imagination. I haven't been sleeping well." It was a lie and we both knew it, but Adam was kind enough not to call me on it.

Was I the only one who could see Huli Jing? No. I shook my head. Mrs. Chang had seen her, too. And now she was dead. Was Huli some kind of portent of death? Was that what awaited me? Or only the people close to me? It didn't matter. I wasn't the type to sit around and wait. If I was going to die, then I'd die hunting.

CHAPTER TWO

"Tell me what you know about Solomon's Seals."

I could tell by Adam's pained expression that he'd hoped I'd forgotten about Finn Logan's suggestion to use the seals to catch the rampaging Shade.

"What I know is that you shouldn't mess with magic," he said. "It's dangerous. Now let me take you home. I'm sure Shaggy would appreciate the company."

I decided not to press the subject. Adam had gone above and beyond, for someone I didn't even date. Far more than I deserved, to tell the truth. Yeah, I knew part of it was just him doing his job, but I wanted to think that he cared at least a little. Besides, if I wanted answers, I needed to go to the source—Finn.

Adam dropped me off at my house. He'd told me to lay low until he got back from the precinct. I figured that was the least I could do, considering all the trouble I'd given him. The message light was blinking on the answering machine, when I stepped through the door. I gave Shaggy's furry head a quick pat, which earned me a tail wag, then hit the play button and strolled into the kitchen.

"Alexa, this is Gloria Jean Manson. The exorcism that

you performed the other day didn't work. Mr. Wiggles is back and seems more agitated than normal. Could you please phone me when you get in? I'm afraid he's going to hurt Mrs. Peabody."

I listened to the dial tone for a few seconds, trying to come up with a way to gently let Gloria down. I couldn't have her getting hurt by this haunt, but in no way could I kill a spectral dog.

The phone rang, interrupting my inner debate. This time it was Adam. "I wanted to make sure that you were okay."

I hesitated, then answered, "I am."

"What's wrong? You haven't seen Huli Jing again. Have you?" There were phones ringing in the background and I could hear papers being shuffled.

"No, nothing like that. I got another call from Gloria. She's still having problems with her gho—drywall."

Adam chuckled. "You can drop the act. I'm not going to bust you for ghost-hunting without a license."

I bit my lip. "Thanks."

The tapping of computer keys came over the line. Slow and methodical, definitely the two-finger method. "What are you going to do?" Adam asked. I could almost picture him searching out the keys as we talked.

My grip on the phone tightened. "I may take a ride out there and see if I can scare it into silence for a while."

He paused. "I thought you never had a problem killing ghosts."

My hesitation was palpable. "I don't, but this is different."

"How?" he asked, genuine curiosity in his voice.

I sighed and ran a hand through my short blond hair. "It just is."

"Hang on a sec." His hand slid over the receiver. I heard muffled voices, but not much conversation. "Sorry about that," he said a minute later.

"No problem."

The voices around him were louder now, chaotically fighting for purchase to be heard over the din. "Listen, I have to get off here. Are you sure that you're going to be okay?" he asked. "I shouldn't be long, a few hours at the most."

I smiled, letting warmth and confidence sink into my voice before answering. "I'll be fine. It won't take long. Besides, I need to get back and do more research. There has to be something I missed on my client list."

"Be careful," he said, his voice suddenly serious.

"I will." I disconnected the call, then phoned Gloria. She picked up on the first ring.

She sounded out of breath like she'd been running around the house. "Alexa, thank goodness it's you."

My senses prickled. "Are you all right?"

"Yes, but I'm not sure Mrs. Peabody will be. Mr. Wiggles has been dive-bombing her for the past five hours. She's peed so many times she doesn't have any urine left. The poor thing is huddled in the corner now and won't stop shaking. Every time I move to comfort her, Mr. Wiggles nips at my ankles."

"I'll be right over." I hung up and walked into the kitchen. It had been a long time since I'd tried to trap a ghost by using salt. Mainly because it rarely worked and didn't actually get them out of the house. I was hoping that Gloria had an extra room that we could drive Mr. Wiggles into temporarily. At least that way, he'd stop terrorizing her and Mrs. Peabody long enough for them to get some rest.

* * * * *

With kosher salt on hand, I drove to Topanga Canyon. Gloria hadn't been exaggerating. Mrs. Peabody looked like she was about to have a doggy nervous breakdown. Her white fluff was matted to her body and her watery eyes bugged out of her head, making her look like a half-drowned, long-haired squirrel. Gloria was still in her pajamas and her pink hair was in disarray.

"I apologize for my less than acceptable appearance."

She worried the edges of her pink and yellow floral silk top, then rubbed her sweaty palms against the matching bottoms. The movement pulled at her pants leg, revealing a pair of fuzzy pink pig slippers and several red welts on her ankles. "I'm afraid it's been a rough day," she said. "I really don't know what has gotten into Mr. Wiggles. He's never behaved this badly."

The temperature in the home was fairly normal, hovering around seventy degrees, but the feel had changed. As I looked around, I couldn't quite put my finger on what was different. It wasn't so much negative as anticipatory. Waiting. But for what? "Gloria, do you have an extra room that you don't use?"

She thought about it for a moment. "I rarely go into the guest bathroom."

"Is it small?"

She nodded.

Thank goodness.

"How many doorways does it have?"

She frowned. "One. Why do you ask?"

"Since I'm having trouble vanquishing Mister—your old dog, I thought the next best thing may be to trap him in a room for a while."

Gloria opened her mouth to say something, but I cut her off before she could speak. "At least until I can come up with a way to permanently remove him."

"Oh my." She pressed a hand to her chest, her expression pensive. "I suppose that will have to do. As long as he doesn't have to stay up there for very long. Mr. Wiggles never liked being alone."

"No," I lied. "He won't have to stay there for long." I'd eventually get someone else to come in and finish the job, but it might take a month or two. That thought didn't do much to ease my conscience.

I took out the ES and turned it on the lowest setting. I put the salt container in my pocket, then grabbed my infrared camera. It didn't take long to spot the dog. He was running back and forth and jumping all over the place. I'd never seen a Shade do that. Maybe it was a dog thing. He kept looking out the windows and appeared to be barking, although I couldn't hear a thing.

I glanced outside, but didn't immediately see anything. I turned back to Gloria. "Are you sure you didn't do anything different?"

"Positive. He's been like this ever since you left."

I supposed that could explain it, but even as the thought crossed my mind I didn't quite believe it. Something had upset the dog. Something outside of the house. I raised the camera and aimed the viewer out the window and slowly panned from left to right. The sun made it impossible to distinguish hot spots.

I pointed the camera back at the dog. He was still watching out the window, not paying a bit of attention to me. "There's nothing there, buddy," I said. He cocked his head and looked over his shoulder at me, his tail wagging much like Shaggy's.

Sometimes I really hated my job. I pressed the button on the electronic scrambler and watched his image quiver, then start to fade. Had I just killed him? I looked around frantically. It took me a second to find him again. He'd moved about five feet behind me and looked perfectly normal for a dead dog. Relief flooded me. That was close.

"Get going." I shooed him up the stairs and pressed the button again.

The dog took off like a shot. With the infrared camera, I followed hot on his doggy heels. An hour later, I'd managed to herd him into the guest bathroom. I spread the kosher salt in front of the doorway, before he could dart out. I backed up and waited, watching him.

He sat a moment, his tongue lolling out of his mouth, then ran for what he thought was freedom. The second he hit the doorway, the dog bounced back, landing on his butt. He tilted his head from side to side, then tried it again only to achieve the same result. He barked soundlessly at the barrier.

The salt was working. But for how long was anyone's guess. The third time Mr. Wiggles approached slowly and sniffed at the door.

I didn't know if dead dogs could still smell things on this plane of existence. If they could, he'd just realized that there was something there. The dog didn't try to break the barrier again. Instead, he walked deeper into the room and curled up on the rug in front of the shower.

"Good boy."

That would at least keep him out of Gloria's pink hair for a while. Maybe even allow Mrs. Peabody to calm down. It was the best I could do. I walked back down the stairs and found Gloria holding a trembling Mrs. Peabody.

She stroked the terrified dog. "Is it done?" she asked.

"Yes, for now. He won't be able to get out of the bathroom unless someone removes the salt. I know it's only temporary. I will do some more reading and see if I can find a permanent solution."

The dog shook violently, nearly propelling her tiny body out of Gloria's grasp. "Well, at least you've saved Mrs. Peabody. I don't think she could've taken much more, the poor dear. Just look at her."

"She's in pretty bad shape, but I'm sure she'll recover quickly. Dogs are like kids, they bounce back fast."

Gloria shook her head. "I don't know. I'm afraid that she might have a heart attack. I've already phoned the vet. He's prescribed a mild sedative. Said if that doesn't work, I'm to bring her in tomorrow and he'd recommend a counselor."

I blinked in surprise. "For you or Mrs. Peabody?"

Gloria arched a pink brow and sniffed. "At least you haven't lost your sense of humor, dear."

I knew some people were gaga over their pets. And I freely admit that I've done some humiliating things to poor Shaggy, but I never once thought about putting him in therapy. Not even after the cone of shame situation.

Gloria patted the dog's head. "Mrs. Peabody can't help it if she has delicate sensibilities."

I just smiled. What else could I do? "I'd better get going. I have some research to do and my roses aren't going to prune themselves." I let her believe that the research was for her haunted terripoo, and then left.

When I pulled into my driveway, I noticed that Adam still wasn't home. Part of me was disappointed, while the other half reminded me not to get too attached. He wouldn't be around forever.

I took Shaggy out for a run, then went into my garden and pruned roses. Sweat dripped down my face, trickling between my shoulder blades. I worked until my fingers ached, allowing my thoughts to wander, but I was no closer to understanding what was happening and why.

Frustrated, I pulled off my gardening gloves and dropped them by the back door as I entered the kitchen. I fed Shaggy and put some chicken noodle soup on, then took a quick shower.

I perused my client records while I ate. I needed to determine if there were any other similarities between my slain clients that everyone, including me, had missed. Pulling out my notes for each case, I scanned the pages. I made a mental note to print from here on out. Not even pharmacists would be able to decipher my scribbles.

The Changs' folder sat next to the Hawkins case, so it would be easier to peruse. Nothing immediately popped out. Neither family was into the occult. There'd been no altars found or haunted items discovered.

Unlike the Changs' haunt, the Hawkinses hadn't experienced routine poltergeist activity. They'd spotted a translucent figure on two occasions and experienced cold spots. Scary, yes. Dangerous, not normally. It had only taken me thirty minutes to dispatch the Shade in the Hawkins's home. That had been three years ago. A follow-up call a week after the initial cleansing showed no new activity. To my knowledge, that hadn't changed.

So why had it started again?

The randomness of the attack ate at me. Had Ryan inadvertently drawn something to him? Doubtful. But he was the right age. Shades loved the young because they could see them and interact. Why hadn't we found his body? Shouldn't it have been there with his parents?

My notes told me no one owned a Talking board. The Changs didn't even have children, so why had they been killed? Were their deaths in any way related to the Hawkins's murders, other than being my clients? Or was that a fluke?

I wasn't sure anymore. I certainly hadn't seen Huli Jing the night my parents died. I would've remembered. Yet it was no coincidence that the bodies were piling up and I was at the center of the maelstrom.

As much as I hated to admit it, I decided it was time to call my other clients and check on them. If they were experiencing new activity, I'd warn them to leave their homes immediately.

By the time I made the sixth call, I knew I had a problem. I'd received two hang-ups and one lawsuit threat. The other two had sounded cheerful until I told them my name. They promptly claimed that I had the wrong number and disconnected the call. Word had obviously gotten around, thanks to all the unwanted media coverage.

I pushed the soup aside and kept dialing.

The final call was the most disturbing of all. I had phoned the Wendel family. The wife's cousin had answered. She informed me that the Wendels had been killed three years ago in a freak accident. I hung up and put a question mark next to their name.

I knew it was possible that the Wendels had died without supernatural help, but I didn't think it was probable. That meant that the first death had occurred long before this pattern emerged. Possibly much longer, since I hadn't been able to reach everyone.

How long had my clients been dying without me knowing about it?

I stared at the list, noting the number of spaces between the Hawkins's case and the Wendels'. There were seven. I then counted the number of spaces between the Wendels and the Changs. There were six.

Seven. Six.

Seven. Six.

My heart began to pound in my chest. It couldn't be that simple, could it? I counted seven more spaces and my fingers landed upon Maria and Jose Gonzalez. There was a chance that all this was unrelated. But there was also the possibility that this was a pattern. A very *familiar* pattern. The same one that had come up on my Talking board all those years ago.

I couldn't risk the Gonzalez's lives, no matter how slim the chance. I'd rather have them kick me out or call the police to arrest me than to ignore my gut and have them end up dead.

I dialed their number, but there was no answer. They could be out. It was a beautiful day. Just because they did not answer didn't mean anything bad had happened. They could be at the park or the zoo or at work, I thought, ignoring the panic rising inside of me. Maybe they were out of town. Would that protect them? I didn't know. No matter where they were, I needed to find them. Needed to be sure they were okay.

I gathered all my equipment, shoving my EMP and ES into my pocket, and headed out the door. It would take me at least an hour to reach West El Segundo Boulevard in Hawthorne, one of the many suburbs in L.A. If this thing was after all my clients, I didn't have a minute to spare.

CHAPTER THREE

The children were playing. Loud sounds of laughter battled the television for attention. The woman was in the kitchen cooking, while the man watched a pigskin being tossed around on the screen.

It waited patiently in the corner, looking for the perfect opportunity to strike. The man might abate its hunger, but not for as long as the children. Their young souls glistened like gold in their brown eyes. Tempting even the most patient.

It listened to their chatter. Watched to see if their dulled senses would flare to life. And still it felt nothing.

Nothing but the ever-present hunger that told it when to feed, so that it may live.

It was about to swoop in for the two tiny morsels, when it sensed the other moving swiftly toward its prey. It raced forward, determined to stop its enemy this time, but it was too late. The other arrived first. Again.

Anger filled it as the cold one swept the children's souls away and removed their bodies right before its eyes. The man hadn't even noticed when the laughter stopped. Nor had he felt the ensuing cold. But he did notice the burning pain that came from having your essence sucked out through your chest. And he did hear his wife calling his name a second before his neck snapped and the world he had so carefully built faded away.

* * * * *

I jerked and my forehead smacked the steering wheel. Wincing, I rubbed at the small knot that had started to form. My body felt weighted and groggy like I'd taken a long, deep nap. But for some reason I couldn't remember falling asleep. I scrubbed a hand over my face and looked outside, expecting to see my house.

It wasn't there.

Neither was my driveway.

I rubbed my eyes and looked again, but I was still parked on an unfamiliar street in a neighborhood I didn't recognize. Where was I? I couldn't remember starting the truck, much less driving. I concentrated, but couldn't recall much of anything beyond grabbing my keys…and the dream. No, not a dream. Another nightmare. I searched for a street name or number.

It scared me that I didn't know where I was or how I'd gotten here.

Most people were at work at this hour. My gaze landed on the nearest house. There was nothing special about its nondescript white siding. It looked much like the others. I was about to dismiss it, when my eyes locked onto the crisp black letters above the front door.

Bienvenido a Casa Gonzalez.

There were a lot of Gonzalezes in the greater Los Angeles area. The odds were that I was sitting outside a stranger's home. But even as the thought crossed my mind, I knew this family had been one of my clients. One of the clients I'd checked on, but had been unable to contact.

A shiver tracked through me as I climbed out of my truck and walked to the front door. No one answered when I rang the doorbell. I glanced at the sedan and SUV in the driveway, then pounded on the door. If I hadn't been listening so intently, I wouldn't have heard the muffled scream. I rushed around the back, while dialing 911 on my cell- phone. I dodged the swing set and toys lying in the yard and raced to the sliding door.

It was locked.

Cupping my hands to the side of my face, I peered inside. I could see Maria Gonzalez leaning against a wall in the living room, clutching her husband, Jose. There was blood down the front of him. And he wasn't moving.

"Shit!" I looked around and found a rock in the flowerbed, then hurled it at the sliding glass door. It shattered, but didn't break. Damn tempered glass. I kicked as hard as I could, knocking a hole in it. The space wasn't big, but I managed to squeeze through.

"It's okay, Maria. I'm coming." She didn't look at me, didn't even acknowledge the sound of glass breaking. Shock had already set in. "I've called the police. Help is on the way."

Maria shook her head and rocked Jose like a frightened child clutching a ragdoll. "It's too late. It's too late," she said, her eyes growing wide with fright. "*Madre de Dios*, Mother of God, *el Diablo es aquí*. The devil is here."

The hair on the back of my neck stood on end and my eyes began to water. My flight or fight response demanded that I get the hell out of there. But I didn't. I couldn't. These were my clients. I was the reason the devil was at their door.

Bypassing the scrambler in my pocket, I stepped deeper into the room and reached for my homemade EMP device. I didn't think. Couldn't think. My body was operating on instinct. I pressed the button, sending out an electromagnetic pulse wave through the house.

A shadow moved up the wall and over the ceiling, staining it with a milky residue. The unnatural movement caught my attention. Shades hated EMP's because they took away their food source. You can't draw energy from dead equipment. The shadow moved again. Was this a Shade or a shadow man?

Shadow men weren't normally affected by my EMP. No one knew for sure what shadow men were, so they garnered their own category in ghost-hunting circles. The electronic scrambler had always worked better on them. This one seemed different, so I held the button down on the EMP.

The shadow shimmered like sunlight on a pond, then disappeared.

Relief hit me and I slumped against the picture-lined wall. We'd won. I couldn't believe it. It took me a beat to realize that Maria was still staring at something across the room. Something that held her undivided attention. She hadn't even seen the shadow. I followed her line of sight.

Ryan Hawkins stood in the middle of the floor, scratches covering every patch of bare skin. He wore blue jeans and a brown T-shirt and had a strange blue-green hat with yellow trim propped haphazardly on his dark head as an afterthought.

Mud caked his face and hands, darkening his fingernails. It was as if he'd dug himself out of a fresh grave. The thought chilled me. A mushroom sprouted from one of his pants pockets and ants crawled over his small bare feet, ducking between his toes, then scurrying back out. He smelled like dirt and rot. A pungent odor that had my gag reflex working overtime.

Ryan had been taken from one of my previous clients. Clients who'd been found dead, murdered in their homes by a Shade I'd tried to vanquish. An Amber Alert had been issued for him, but the cops had assumed the worst. What was he doing here? How had he gotten to the Gonzalez home of all places?

For a moment all I could do was stare. I was so shocked to see him alive that I forgot all about the horror around me, forgot about everything. "Maria, what is Ryan doing here?" My gaze remained transfixed on the missing child. He shouldn't be here. He didn't belong.

Ryan didn't look at me. He continued to stare at Maria. She whimpered and clutched Jose tighter. "He is *Diablo*. The devil, I say. Keep him away. He cannot have Jose." She crossed herself and began to rock harder. Tears streamed down her rounded face, streaking her cinnamon-colored cheeks.

Pleas for God and her mother grew toward a crescendo. She gripped Jose and fingered the cross around her neck. I couldn't listen any longer. Her cries ripped at my heart.

"I won't let him take Jose." I inched closer. I needed to get between them. The movement finally seemed to get Ryan's attention.

It was only when he looked directly at me, showing me the endless black pits that served as his eyes, that I realized I wasn't staring at Ryan Hawkins at all. I was looking at a creature much like Huli Jing, the demon who'd put me through a door a few days ago and branded my skin with her handprint.

Fear grasped me and refused to let go. My limbs shook as I prepared to defend Maria Gonzalez. "What have you done with Ryan?" I asked the creature masquerading as a child. I couldn't imagine the torment the child had gone through when confronted by this abomination.

"He is out of your reach," his voice rasped like he'd been gargling rocks.

What did he mean by that? "Where is he?"

If Ryan was still alive, I needed to find him, get him to safety. It would take years of counseling to get him past this ordeal.

"Gone!" it hissed.

I flinched at the ferocity of that single word. "Gone where?"

His gray face became mottled. "I do not have time for these questions."

"Can you at least tell me your name?" I took another step

toward Maria.

There was an air of disapproval emanating from him, like I'd somehow insulted him by asking his name, but I wasn't about to call him Ryan. This wasn't Ryan.

"I am known by many names, but most Beings here call me Kayeri." He waited for some kind of reaction.

It didn't come. His name meant *nothing* to me.

His expression turned thunderous as anger threaded through his tiny body. "I'm surprised that you do not recognize me, Gosling," he snarled.

I'd heard that term before. Huli had used it. Was this her? The last time I'd seen her, she'd been a five to seven year old Asian girl. Could demons change sex? I thought about asking, but took one look at his expression and changed my mind.

"Should I recognize you?" I asked, taking a long hard look at him. "As far as I know, we haven't met. I don't even know *what* you are." But I could guess.

The fake Ryan frowned in what looked to be confusion, then his expression slowly cleared. I half expected him to call me a liar. But I wasn't lying. I really didn't know what I was dealing with.

"No matter." Kayeri shook his head. "Though rare, these things happen. You will not obstruct me from completing my duty."

We'd see about that, I thought.

Maria cried out and tightened her chokehold on Jose. If he weren't already dead, he would be now. No way could he breathe with that death grip around his neck.

It took supreme effort, but I managed to keep my voice steady. "What duty? Why are you here? These people haven't done anything to you." Could you reason with a demon? I didn't know, but I was willing to give anything a shot.

He glared at me. "It is you who should not be here, Gosling. The souls are all gone, except for hers." He pointed at Maria. "I will not let you have it. 'Tis mine."

What did it mean by the souls were all gone? And why was he worried about me getting them? I didn't want anyone's soul. And I certainly hadn't come to get Maria's soul, but I wasn't about to let a demon have it either. The thought went against everything I'd ever read.

"I can assure you that I'm here to save Maria—from you."

"You lie!" he bellowed and took an intimidating step forward. The windows shook, threatening to shatter.

Despite his diminutive size, I stepped back. "I do not," I croaked.

He glared venomously.

"Not about this, I don't," I amended.

Before I could ask more questions he said, "Enough talk."

I crept closer to the Gonzalezes. A siren wailed in the distance. Help was almost here. I just had to keep Ryan/Kayeri busy until they arrived. It was the only way Maria would survive.

He took another menacing step. Pretty impressive display for a dead seven-year-old kid.

"You can't have her, demon. That is what you are, isn't it?" I squared off to face him. Not the brightest of ideas, but I had little choice. "Leave now and I won't hurt you." The bluff came out confident. I just had to pray he wouldn't call me on it.

My grip tightened on the EMP and ES. I hoped that combined they'd actually do some damage or at least distract him until help arrived. I didn't need another handprint burned into me. The one I had already clashed with the birthmark on my hip.

Ryan threw his head back and laughed. "You cannot hurt me with mortal weapons, Gosling."

That's what I was afraid of, since my equipment had only left scratches on Huli Jing, but I couldn't back down now.

Our lives were on the line. "Let's test that theory." I cranked the EMP dial to ten, holding my thumb above the button, all but daring him to come closer.

His gaze grew even colder and the windows began to frost. My breath formed white clouds before my face. "Press that and you'll be sorry," he snarled.

"I already am," I said. "But I'm not half as sorry as you're going to be, if you don't get out of here." It was an empty threat. I was pretty sure he knew it, too, but Kayeri hadn't moved. "I'm surprised a demon is afraid of a little EMP device," I taunted, purposely trying to piss him off so his attention stayed on me and not Maria. I shouldn't have worried.

Flames rose behind his eyelids.

I'd been anticipating that, but not the overwhelming fear that followed. My bowels threatened to empty and I could barely swallow.

He raised his tiny hands. "Some goslings insist on learning the hard way. Next time I won't be so lenient."

Pressure in the room began to build. I had to clear my ears just to equalize them. Maria's wails continued. Her brown eyes were open, but there was no one home.

I gritted my teeth against the pain and said, "Stop it, you're hurting her."

"The damage to her has already been done," he said. "I'm here to alleviate her suffering."

I snorted. "Somehow I doubt that."

Mentally, Maria had gone somewhere else. Trouble was, I needed her with me when it came time to run.

"Stay with me, Maria. Help is coming." I searched frantically for an escape route. The closest exit was the one I'd created through the sliding door. It wasn't big enough for both of us.

"She's mine now," Kayeri said.

I pressed the EMP button and the ES. "Over my dead body."

"As you wish," he said.

A second later something invisible hit me. Hard. As if I'd caught the backdraft from an explosion, I was lifted off my feet and propelled into the kitchen. I crashed into the center island. My lungs deflated as I hit the wood and marble, leaving me gasping for air. I heard bones crack and pain shot through my shoulder. A wave of nausea followed. I had to swallow repeatedly to keep from throwing up.

Maria screamed long and loud. So did Ryan. Blood trickled out of my ears and onto the floor. That couldn't be good. My eyes lost focus. The screams abruptly cut off. A burping gurgle followed, then silence returned.

"Maria." I croaked, my voice barely above a whisper.

I tried to see into the other room, but my head refused to turn and my vision wasn't cooperating. I lay there in helpless disarray, twitching from the aftershocks reverberating through my body. My lids grew heavy. I couldn't seem to keep them open. The room dimmed, then I saw nothing at all.

Chapter Four

"Ms. Dawn, can you hear me?"

I awoke with a start and found a flashlight shining in my face. A semicircle of police stood around me, staring down at my crumpled form. I swatted at the light or at least I tried to, but my arm wasn't cooperating. An officer I didn't recognize moved the beam and the spots slowly faded from my eyes.

"Where am I?"

"Stay still," he said. "We haven't assessed your injuries yet."

Adam Grayson pushed his way through the crowd. "Is she all right?"

Adam was my new neighbor. He also happened to be a lead detective. Why was he here? And why did he look so worried?

"We won't know until we get her to the hospital. She came to a second ago, but she doesn't know where she is," the officer said.

Adam looked at me, his face twisted in pain. "Alexa, do you remember me?"

That was a stupid question. "Yes," I said.

"What happened here?" he asked.

Nothing looked familiar. This wasn't my house. "Where's here? I don't know where I am."

"You're at the Gonzalez residence," Adam said. "Remember them?"

Shards of images flashed in my mind. They didn't make sense. I concentrated harder, ignoring the pain it brought. The images blurred, then slowly formed a clear picture. My eyes widened. "Where's Maria? Did you take her to the hospital?"

Adam's gaze fell away and he shook his head, tousling his already mussed hair. "Maria's dead. So is Jose. The kids are missing, just like in the Hawkins case."

"No, that's not possible. She was alive a few minutes ago." The numbers swam as I looked at my watch. "How long have I been here?"

"We aren't sure. Couldn't have been very long, since it took less than twelve minutes for the police to get here."

That's right. I'd phoned the police before I broke into the house.

Minutes had seemed like an eternity, while staring at the... My brow furrowed. "Where's Ryan?" I tried to sit up, but my shoulder hurt too much. I gasped in pain and fell back.

Adam's frown deepened. "Don't you mean Manuel?"

Did I mean Manuel? I shook my head. Pain shot through my temple and I grimaced. I waited for it to fade, then forced myself to concentrate. Who had I seen? Ryan's rumpled image wavered in my mind. "Ryan Hawkins is here. I saw him." I clutched Adam's shirt. "You have to find him."

He held me immobile. "You need to stay still until the ambulance arrives. I think you have a concussion," he said.

I knew something was cracked, but it wasn't my head. I might be somewhat confused, but not about seeing...the demon. My heart accelerated. I frantically glanced around, but couldn't see anything other than the cops surrounding me. "You don't understand."

"We need you to tell us what happened here." Adam gently pushed me back down. "Right now, you are our only lead. Our only witness." *And prime suspect—again.*

Desperation clawed at my throat. "Maria is alive. She has to be. Or all this was for nothing." I indicated to my broken body.

Adam touched my face. "Alexa, you're the sole survivor."

"No! No! You're wrong," I gasped, tightening my hold on his shirt. "Nothing moves that fast. He couldn't have got to her."

"Lex, you're not making sense." Adam's face closed. "Who are you talking about?"

My fingers closed on his collar. "Ryan." I shook him. "He was in the house when I got here. I saw him."

Adam gave me a brittle smile. "You couldn't have."

"I know what I saw, Adam. It was Ryan Hawkins, except Ryan wasn't really Ryan anymore. He was a demon like Huli Jing."

He pried my fingers off. "You need to relax. You have a nasty bump on your head."

"Don't tell me to relax." My voice rose until I was shouting. "You don't know what he's capable of. You didn't see him."

Sadness tinged Adam's face. "Yes, I did. We found Ryan buried in the backyard next to the swing set under a mushroom patch. There's a team out there now, trying to see if the Gonzalezes' two children are with him."

"I'm telling you I saw him. He was in the house, standing right over there." I pointed toward the living room. "He was after Maria's soul. I tried to stop him, but he was too strong."

"She's lost it," I heard someone in the group murmur.

"Tell that medic to get a move on," Adam shouted. "And someone get me some ice."

Adam laid a makeshift ice pack against my temple. The

coolness felt good on my fevered skin. "Why do they keep taking the kids? Eva is only nine years old and poor Manuel is five. They have to be here. Have you checked in their closets and under their beds? What about the neighbors?"

"Someone is canvassing the neighborhood as we speak. If they're anywhere around, we'll find them." Adam brushed the hair off my forehead. "I know this is difficult, but the preliminary investigation is looking like a murder-suicide. It's rare that the wife is the one to do this sort of thing, but it does happen. And when it does, they normally kill the kids, too."

My brow furrowed. "Murder-suicide? What are you talking about? You can't seriously believe that. Not after everything I—" I cut myself off. He already thought I'd bumped my head hard enough to imagine Ryan in the house. If I started babbling about shadows climbing walls and premonitory visions, they'd hold me over for psychiatric observation and Adam would sign the papers himself. But I knew what I had seen, even if no one believed me.

Radios crackled, causing a cacophony of sound in the small space. Sirens wailed as more units closed in on the scene. They could call out every cop on the force and it wouldn't help them with this case.

"Alexa, are you still with me?" Adam asked.

My eyelids fluttered as I tried to focus on his face. "Yes."

"The medical examiner said that it's clear by the liver temps that Jose has been dead at least a couple of hours. Maria was the only one home until you arrived."

Forgetting all about my injury, I shook my head in denial. Shards of pain knifed me. "Maria and Jose are Catholic. There's no way they would commit murder, much less suicide. It's a mortal sin."

"How long has it been since you last saw the Gonzalez family, Alexa?"

I went to shrug and pain radiated across my chest. "I don't remember. Three years maybe."

"A lot can happen in that time period. One of them probably attacked you, when you weren't looking."

It hadn't been the Gonzalezes who attacked me. I was sure of that, even if I couldn't recall the exact moment of impact. It had been the thing inside of Ryan. I'd made him angry. But it would take more than my word to convince the cops that my attacker was the kid lying in the shallow grave out in the backyard next to the swing set.

"Why did you come here anyway?" Adam asked.

My throat burned. "I was checking on *all* my old clients. After what happened to the Changs and the Hawkins' family, I wanted to make sure that everyone else was okay."

"Why didn't you call first?" he asked. "It would've been easier than driving thirty miles."

Our gazes met. "I did phone. They didn't answer."

His expression grew serious, but I could tell it was fueled by concern. "You were damn lucky that you didn't end up like the Gonzalezes."

"I know," I croaked.

Adam ran a hand over his face and sighed. "I guess I'm going to have to keep a closer eye on you. You seem to get into trouble when I'm not around."

I didn't think Adam was joking, but I decided to pretend that he was, so I laughed. The paramedics entered the kitchen. They consisted of a man and a woman team, who didn't hesitate to order the cops back so that they could have room to work. The blond woman gave me a cursory examination, while her partner relayed the findings to the hospital. A few minutes later, they plopped me onto a wobbly gurney and wheeled me out into a media frenzy.

Clicks and flashes filled the air, as the press and everyone with a cell-phone tried to capture my image. Quite a crowd had gathered around the Gonzalez home. The only thing that kept them at bay was a thin strip of crime scene tape.

When we got near the ambulance, I told them that I didn't want to be taken to the hospital. I was a fast healer and there wasn't much the doctors could do for a cracked collarbone beyond putting a sling on me.

"We'll have to check with the detective," the woman said, while continuing to track my vitals.

When the male EMT left to talk to Adam, I noticed a tall dark-haired man dressed in a long black duster, standing nearby. I'd seen him before. He'd been at the Changs' crime scene. Or at least I was pretty sure that he'd been there. He'd been too far away to get a clear look and had disappeared before I'd had a chance to move closer.

The female paramedic finished her work. I asked her to give me a waiver. The waiver meant that they couldn't be held accountable if I keeled over and died. I needed to sign it before the male EMT returned because I had a feeling Adam wouldn't agree with my decision. She encouraged me one last time to seek medical attention. I told her I would, to quiet her protests.

Adam was still inside the Gonzalez home, mapping out the crime scene, so I hobbled over to where the man stood. He didn't bother to pretend that he hadn't been watching me. Instead, his brown gaze intensified as I neared.

"Why are you here?" My eyes narrowed. "You don't strike me as one of those freaks that go from crime scene to crime scene to try to catch a glimpse of the bodies," I said, tactful as always.

If he considered my words provocative, he didn't let on. If anything, he looked amused. The man was incredibly tall. At five foot seven, I'm not exactly short, but I had to crane my neck to get a good look at his face. When I did, my breath caught in my throat.

Living in L.A. you see a fair share of gorgeous people. But no actor on the silver screen could touch this man in the looks department. Straight hair the color of night hung past his broad shoulders. A shadow of stubble brushed his strong jaw, framing lips that were made for erotic fantasies.

Earthy and primal, his skin glowed a deep golden brown.

There were no lines on his face to indicate his age, but something about his eyes told me that he was older than he appeared.

I continued to gather details about him. I had a feeling I'd need them at some point. "Aren't you going to say anything?"

He remained silent and simply arched a brow.

"Suit yourself." I turned to leave, but his response stopped me cold.

"We have much in common, you and I," he said in a rumbling baritone that I felt more than heard. He shifted casually, causing a ripple to move through the fabric of his black duster. "We are both hunters. I seek what you seek."

Not exactly the response I'd expected, but he had my full attention. That didn't mean I was ready to show him my hand. Instead, I played coy. He could always turn out to be a crackpot. There are a lot of them on the west coast and not all of them live out of grocery carts.

"What exactly do you hunt in Los Angeles? It's not like there's a lot of wild game running about."

"Other-worlders and rogue seraphs." He shrugged. "Whatever they tell me to pursue." His lips twitched in amusement.

"They who?"

All traces of humor fled. "That's confidential."

Considering you needed a license to hunt Shades, I couldn't really fault him for being paranoid. I wouldn't disclose my client information either. Discretion was the only way you kept working. "Is a seraph a fancy word for Shade or are you talking about—demons?" I asked.

He cocked his head and grinned, glancing at my bandaged shoulder. "How does that feel?" he asked, changing the subject.

"Just peachy, Mister...Mister..." I felt a sharp pain in the side of my temple and sucked in a breath. My hand automatically moved to my head and I swayed on my feet.

He reached out to steady me. My arm tingled where he'd touched. He must've felt it, too, because he drew back and rubbed his hand over his shirt. "I am called Gabriel...among other things." His gaze restlessly scanned the crowd.

"Well, Gabriel among other things, I'm Alexa Dawn."

His lips quirked. "I know. 'Tis a pleasure to finally meet. You may call me Gabe."

Finally? Finally implied he'd been waiting.

I started to ask how he'd heard of me, then remembered the reporters at the two previous crime scenes. Of course he knew who I was; the entire city of Los Angeles knew me now. I'd been all over the news. They'd made me famous, or more like infamous. Not that many people understood the difference these days.

"How did you hear about this crime?" I looked at the gathering crowd. A few people snapped pictures with their phones. "Do you listen to police scanners or did you catch the video online?"

Gabe gave me a wry smile. "I'm afraid that technology and I don't get along," he said.

"Must make it difficult to hunt Shades."

He shook his head, sending a swatch of silky-looking hair into eyes. He casually brushed it aside. "Not really. Please allow me." He touched my shoulder. Warmth spread through my body. A second later, something popped.

"Ouch." Pain radiated for a moment, then dulled. "What did you do?"

"Helped," he said nonchalantly, not in the least concerned about my discomfort or confusion.

I rolled my shoulder. There was a slight ache, but that was about all. Even my head had stopped throbbing. "Did you somehow hypnotize me into believing that I'm better?"

"Something like that," he said, without expanding upon his answer.

"You say we're hunting the same thing. How can you do that without equipment?" If he had a way to kill demons, I needed to know about it.

"I have a far more effective way of finding other-worlders than your primitive technology."

"Really? What do you use? Some kind of divination tool?" I asked.

If he had something more effective to hunt Shades with, perhaps it would help me find the one I'd been seeking.

"My methods are unimportant," Gabe said.

Just what I thought. He was full of it. I should've known by looking at him that he was a poser. I didn't have time to deal with a Harry Dresden wannabe. He probably wasn't even a hunter.

Another crime scene unit van pulled up in front of the house. Gabe's eyes darkened. "I shall be hunting this one alone," he said, more to himself than to me.

"One?" I snorted. "You think one did that. You may want to do a recount. You're off by two."

Gabe frowned in confusion, then closed his eyes and inhaled deeply through his nose. He looked at me, when he exhaled. "No, there is only one. 'Tis you who are mistaken."

I crossed my arms over my chest. "Wrong again, Tonto. There are three and counting. I've seen them. Why do you think I'm in bandages? And I've got another news flash for you, this Lone Ranger is not about to step aside and let you do her job for her."

There was no way that I'd allow him to catch the Shade that I'd been hunting for seven years. Much less take out the demons terrorizing my clients. That was my job even if I wasn't sure how I'd accomplish it.

He smiled and brushed my cheek with a fingertip. It was a simple gesture not meant to ensnare. But before I could stop myself, I leaned into his caress. I couldn't seem to stop myself. Something flashed in Gabe's dark eyes as he tenderly cupped my face. He stepped forward and the heat from his body enveloped me, making me even more lethargic. Noises faded. The world around us dropped away as he held me.

"You should feel better now," he said softly, stroking my lower lip with the pad of his thumb.

His words penetrated the strange veil that had fallen over me. I jerked back and felt my face heat with embarrassment as I realized what I'd been doing. I may have been traumatized, but that was no excuse to curl up against the first guy who offered comfort.

Gabe stared at me and I felt the strange pull again. This time I stepped away before I could act. His brow arched, his surprise clear, but he said nothing. I tried to formulate an excuse, but "Sorry my head injury made me want to rub against you" sounded lame. So I kept quiet. I may not act upon my raging hormones, but I definitely had them.

"Test your injury," Gabe said, as if nothing had happened, but his eyes glittered in amusement.

I rolled my shoulder again and felt nothing other than the flex of the muscle beneath my skin.

"Now move your head," he said.

I did, then I felt the spot. The pain was completely gone. Even the lump had disappeared. "How did you do that?"

Before Gabe could answer, Adam called my name.

I turned to see him slowly making his way through the crowd. He was staring at the closed ambulance door with a frown on his face. "I'll be right back," I said to Gabe without looking, then met Adam halfway.

His gaze lingered on my bandages. "You were supposed to be going to the hospital," Adam said.

"There isn't anything they can do for me. They checked my head and told me they didn't think I had a concussion. I might have a cracked collarbone, but it's feeling better now—thanks to Gabe."

"Thanks to who?" Adam asked.

"Gabe." I pointed over my shoulder. It wasn't like he could miss him in the crowd.

Adam's stormy eyes narrowed and pink slashed his

cheeks. "Who's Gabe?" There was a bite to his words

"He's—" I couldn't tell him that Gabe was a hunter, since I wasn't certain he was licensed. I didn't want to get Gabe in trouble, if I could avoid it. "He's some guy I just met."

"You let a stranger touch you?" Adam made it sound like Gabe had been groping me on the sidewalk.

"It wasn't like that," I said defensively.

Why had I let a stranger touch me? I wasn't a touchy feely kind of person. I'd never been one for public displays of affection. Nor had I ever let anyone openly examine me. Maybe I was still in shock about the Gonzalezes' murders.

"We were just talking." Unease squirmed its way through me.

Adam's brow furrowed, shadowing his blue eyes. "At least tell me that he's a doctor?"

I shook my head. "I don't think so. Not in the traditional sense anyway."

He reached for my hand and tugged me toward him protectively. "Then I'm taking you to the hospital."

The warmth of his frame felt good against my suddenly chilled bones. I could've told him that I'd already signed the waiver. Instead, I said, "Okay." And snuggled closer. "I really am feeling much better. I don't know what he did, but whatever it was worked."

"I still want you to get checked out." Adam peered past me and his eyes narrowed. "Did you happen to catch Gabe's last name?"

"No, it never came up." I scowled at him, then stepped out of his arms. "What's with the interrogation? If you have questions for Gabe, then ask him yourself."

"I'd love to, where is he?" Adam asked.

I turned to scan the crowd, but Gabe was gone. "I swear he was standing right over there." I pointed to the last spot I'd seen him in.

Adam's face went from tense to deeply concerned. "Like

you saw Ryan Hawkins?"

He didn't believe me. I could see it in his eyes. I knew what I'd seen—and felt. I wasn't making Gabe up. And I certainly hadn't made up Ryan Hawkins.

Adam must have read the desperation in my expression because he said, "Listen, Alexa, I'm sure he was here. But if he was on the up-and-up, why did he leave in such a hurry?"

Why indeed? A sleek black sports car sped past with its windows down and radio blaring. I caught a glimpse of long dark hair, whipping in the wind, and the sleeve of a black coat.

"Was that him?" Adam stood on his toes and squinted at the rear of the car.

It had looked like him, but he'd gone by so fast I couldn't be sure. "I think so. Did you get the plate number?"

Adam stared for a few seconds, then slowly shook his head. "The Porsche didn't have any plates."

I laughed. "Why am I not surprised?"

CHAPTER FIVE

The sun was setting, when the head of the Paranormal Friends Society phoned the next day. I'd just stepped into the house, carrying a handful of yellow roses from my garden. Some people have a green thumb. I have two of them and eight green fingers to boot. I didn't even have to water my plants and they still grew. Impressive, considering L.A. had pretty much been in a drought for the last ten to fifteen years.

I set the flowers in the sink and grabbed the cordless on the third ring. "What's up, Finn?" I asked.

"I think I should be asking you that," Finn said, with feigned cheer.

I paused. "Why?" Finn Logan was never perky. He detested perky people, equating them to sea sponges. Said they absorbed the life force of those around them.

"Because you promised you'd keep us apprised of the haunt and we haven't heard from you. If it weren't for the news reports flashing your face poking out the back of an ambulance, we'd have no idea what you were up to. You are part of this group, you know." Finn hid his concern well, but I still heard it.

I opened the cabinets, looking for a vase. One appeared

behind door number four. "If you've seen the news, then you know I've been a little busy. But thanks for your concern."

"I'm not concerned," he said hastily. "I just don't want to see the Paranormal Friends Society's reputation damaged due to one of its member's indiscretions."

Indiscretions? What did he mean by that?

"I'm touched, Finn. Really." Sarcasm tinged my voice as I set the vase on the counter.

"Stephen has told me all about your visits to the cop's house," Finn said.

I'd dated Stephen Reynolds for a few months. I wasn't even sure if it was long enough to warrant the term ex-boyfriend. Was Stephen stalking me? How else would he know about my visits to Adam's house?

"When did Stephen tell you that?" I asked innocently.

Finn was too smart to let the details slip. "Doesn't matter, you just confirmed it," he said. "I have to say, Lex, I'm a little surprised that you're helping the police."

I slipped the phone to the crook of my neck, then hacked at the flower stems, instead of trimming them neatly. "My clients are dying, Finn. What would you have me do? Ignore them?"

He hesitated. "I suppose not."

"You're a real humanitarian. So does this phone call have a point or did you just call to harass me?" I asked.

"No need to get witchy," Finn said. "This is a professional call. I thought you should know that Stephen has been following up on these haunts. He thinks he may have found something. Hasn't told me what yet. I know you're not on the best of terms, but you may want to phone him."

I stilled. "What do you mean he's been following up?" Dread settled into my gut as I awaited his answer.

Drawers opened and closed as Finn searched for something. "He's been doing some digging into the past and thinks the whole thing might have started in your old house in Orange County."

My stomach dropped to my knees. How had he found out? My parents' deaths were listed as unsolved homicides. Nothing should've led back to them. "What exactly does Stephen think he's found?"

There was a pause in the line. "Like I said, he hasn't told me yet. Forewarned is forearmed and all that. This call is just to give you a heads-up."

"Thanks." Maybe it wasn't as bad as I thought. Maybe Stephen was still at the research stage or maybe he was using Finn to fish for information. I started to hang up, but stopped short. "Hey Finn, you still there?"

He sounded distracted when he said, "Yes."

"Stephen isn't investigating the murder sites, right? I asked him to stay away until the police solved these latest ones. He's kept his word. Right?"

Finn hesitated. I knew he was deciding how much he should tell me, but right now I needed the truth. Stephen's life hung in the balance.

"Spill it," I said.

There was another pause. "He's staying out of trouble like a good investigator should," he said, then hung up.

He hadn't really given me a straight answer and we both knew it. I debated whether to phone back, but suspected Finn wouldn't pick up if I did. I hated the idea that Stephen was looking into my past, but I'd rather have him invading my childhood than stalking me now like he seemed to be doing. What was he looking for?

It wasn't like I had anything to hide, except maybe the fact that I was the reason my parents were dead. Other than that, my conscience was clear. Of course on paper it would just say unsolved double homicide just like the current crime scenes.

I didn't want to call Stephen. He'd consider the gesture encouragement. But if Finn was right, then I had to warn him again. I picked up the receiver and started to dial, then put it back down. Now that I'd figured out the killer's or killers' pattern, it was doubtful that Stephen would get into any real trouble. After all, he'd be checking out the old scenes where the killer had already struck, not who was next on my client list.

I kept my clients' names alphabetized. With the Gonzalezes dead, that left the seventh client down next in line for a spectral visit. The thought that I should inform Adam popped into my head. I squashed it quickly.

He hadn't been able to see Huli Jing and he hadn't believed me about Ryan Hawkins. I was pretty sure he'd been humoring me about Gabriel. At least until he caught a glimpse of him.

My theory about the killer was just that—a theory. I needed to present facts to Adam. I went back to my records and began to slowly count down the list of names. When I reached seven, I lifted my finger to read the name. My heart dropped.

Oh no, not her. Not Gloria Jean.

* * * * *

It slipped into the house where the old woman sat in the parlor, clutching photographs, her mind trapped in the past. The smile on her face spoke of happier times. She would be easy to devour. Defenseless in this old home that smelled so much like a tomb.

It wandered through the halls, listening to the sounds imbedded in the pink walls. Whispers permeated the silence. Along with something else it couldn't quit identify. Dismissing the odd signature, it searched the rooms to ensure their privacy.

Descending the stairs with all the time in the world, it entered the parlor. The woman hadn't noticed its presence. Yet. But she would. It approached on a breeze. Warmth surrounding it. A hand reached out and touched her candy-colored hair.

She stirred.

Then screamed.

A tiny white dog jumped out of her arms and scurried under the couch. The smell of urine and feces followed.

It reached for her neck, but before it could clasp her throat and begin to feed something rose out of the darkness. Something swift and small with sharp white teeth.

Growls filled the air.

It stepped back, releasing the woman and glanced around for the source of the threat. A bite was delivered. Then another. And another. Its hands cleaved the air, but struck nothing. The force of the attack grew with each snap of insistent jaws.

Unable to see the furry assailant, it had no choice but to flee.

* * * * *

All hell was breaking loose at Gloria Jean Manson's house when I arrived. I rushed through the door, not bothering to knock. Gloria was huddled in a corner holding Mrs. Peabody, who whimpered in her arms. Her burgundy curtains had been ripped and the rods snapped, then tossed onto the carpet.

Glass shattered in the other room. I couldn't see what was going on, but there appeared to be a chase taking place. Following the path of destruction, I stepped on Mr. Wiggles's jingle ball and nearly fell on my butt. I reached down and picked it up as the side table flipped, sending its spindly legs skyward like an overturned turtle.

"Gloria, what's happening?" I screamed over the commotion.

"I'm not sure." She squeezed Mrs. Peabody until her doggy eyes bulged. "A black shadow came after me. I thought I heard Mr. Wiggles bark. It happens sometimes, just not very often. Then all heck broke loose. He didn't go after Mrs. Peabody. Instead, he tore through the house after the shadow." She trembled. "I've never seen him this worked up. Do you think he's channeling a pit bull?"

"Dogs can't channel spirits." At least I didn't think so. I shook my head and went to where she cowered. "It's going to be all right. I know it's scary."

Her gaze left the chaos to fasten on mine. "I am *not* scared of Mr. Wiggles." She sounded insulted. "It's what he's chasing that has me worried. The only time he ever behaved like this was when—" She broke off, frowning.

"When what?" I asked.

Her thin lip quivered. She pulled out a pink handkerchief from her pocket and sniffled. "When he was protecting me from a burglar."

It wasn't a burglar that Mr. Wiggles attacked tonight. He was after something far worse. My gaze tracked the chaos in the room. The place was in such a shambles that I couldn't tell who was winning. I prayed that I was right and that it was Mr. Wiggles. Thank goodness I hadn't forced him from the home, when Gloria hired me to get rid of him. He was the only reason she was still alive.

A thud hit the front door. Gloria and I jumped. What now? I glanced over my shoulder in time to see Adam bursting through the door. He ducked as a plate sailed past his head and landed on the front porch.

"What are you doing here?" I asked, relieved to see him even though I shouldn't be. How was I going to protect them both?

"I followed you." He took the destruction around him in with one glance. "What is going on?"

Before I could answer, Adam's expression changed and his eyes widened. He took a step back, his hands rising in defense.

"Adam, what is it?" I hadn't had time to grab my equipment, so the best I could do was improvise. Of course, that would only work if Gloria had a battery-operated radio and a strong signal from the pop stations.

"We need to get out of here now," he said, without glancing our way. "Come on. Move it," he shouted as a chair flew at him.

I didn't need to be asked twice. I grabbed Gloria's hand and yanked her to her feet. The fury in the house seemed suddenly directed at Adam and I couldn't do anything about it until I got Gloria to safety. She never released Mrs. Peabody, who'd been so scared that she'd urinated down the front of Gloria's pink polyester pants.

Adam reached for me without looking. His eyes remained firmly on the fight in front of us. And there was no doubt a brawl was occurring. Furniture continued to topple, picture frames cracked, curtains tore into strips, and the corpses of several chairs lay in splinters.

The second Adam's hand touched mine, the disturbance stopped. We all froze in place. Afraid to move. Afraid to breathe for fear it would start all over again. Gloria was the first to speak. She pulled her hand free and glanced around at the mess.

"Is it over?" she asked.

I scanned the chaos. "I don't know," I answered truthfully.

Her normally steely sharp eyes filled with moisture. "Is Mr. Wiggles okay?"

"I'm sure he's fine." I leaned close to her ear, so that only she could hear me. "How did he get out of the bathroom?" I asked.

"I forgot about the salt, when I was vacuuming," she said.

Thank goodness she had or her body would've been found like the others.

"Why don't you go on outside, Alexa, and take the little dog with you. I'll help Ms. Manson." Adam stepped past me and put his arm around Gloria's shoulders.

I didn't argue because there wasn't anything I could do here. Mrs. Peabody squirmed in my hands a moment before settling. I still couldn't believe that Gloria had survived an encounter with the Shade that had terrorized me. All she had was two yapper dogs and one of those was dead.

I thought about Mr. Wiggles and Gloria's question. I didn't see how there was any way he could've made it out of the fight unharmed. But I hadn't wanted to tell her that. The eighty-something year old had been through enough already.

I heard Adam murmuring in Gloria's ear. At first his words didn't make sense. Then eventually they registered. He was saying that he'll be fine. He was fine. And would be waiting for her, when she came back home.

It sounded like he was talking about Mr. Wiggles. But how could he be? Adam knew nothing about the details of this case. His cell-phone rang. He reached into his pocket one-handed and retrieved it.

"Grayson." He listened intently. "Could you repeat that?" A second later his gaze fell on me. There was compassion and something else in his eyes that looked suspiciously like pain. "Are you absolutely certain?" He nodded. "Okay. We'll be there in less than an hour."

"What is it?" My heart sank.

He looked at Mrs. Peabody. "Let's get Gloria settled in the hotel down the road first, then I'll tell you everything."

Gloria pulled away from him. "Don't worry about me. I've survived things far scarier than a ghost attack. I hope Mr. Wiggles gave him a good nip on the bottom."

"He did," Adam said, then added, "if the destruction is any indication."

I ignored the rock that had settled in the pit of my stomach.

"I think," she said turning to me. "If you don't mind, I'll just let him live here."

My mind was on Adam's phone call, so I didn't immediately follow. "Who?"

"Do keep up, Alexa. Mr. Wiggles, of course. I think he more than earned the right to stay, tonight. Don't you?" she asked.

I smiled. "Yes, I do believe he has." I handed Mrs. Peabody to Gloria.

She stroked the dog's head. "Your check will arrive in a couple of days," she said.

I stared at her in confusion. I hadn't done anything other than deceive her. "But I didn't finish the job."

"I know," she said. "Thank you." Gloria tucked the dog under her arm and smiled at Adam. "And thank you, young man, for everything. If I were only forty-five years younger, I'd steal you away from this one." She nodded in my direction.

"We aren't—" I started to say a couple, but stopped. I wasn't sure what Adam and I were anymore. We'd started out as neighbors and adversaries. Now, we were more like partners with potential benefits.

Gloria winked at Adam. He grinned back, his blue eyes twinkling. "Well, I believe that's my cue to be on my way." Gloria reached into her pocket for her keys.

"We can take you to the hotel," I said.

"Not necessary. I keep an overnight bag in the trunk of my car just in case." She wagged her eyebrows. "Besides, I've been taking care of myself for more years than you've been breathing on this planet." She walked a short distance to her garage, then piled into a Mercedes. Gloria backed out and stopped. Mrs. Peabody was perched on her lap. "I don't know how you knew that I needed help, but thanks for coming when you did," she said, then pulled away, leaving Adam and I standing in the driveway.

"She's quite a lady," he said.

I watched Gloria drive out of sight, dread growing by the minute. "Yes, she is," I said. "Now tell me what's going on."

Adam's cheerful expression faded. "I think you may want to sit down."

"If it's all the same to you, I'll take the bad news standing."

He grasped my hand. "Stephen Reynolds was found dead thirty minutes ago."

Chapter Six

I couldn't have heard him right. "Excuse me," I said.

"Stephen is dead," Adam repeated.

That wasn't possible. The Shade was here with Gloria and me. I'd figured out where it would strike next. I had uncovered the pattern and arrived in time to save her.

"You have to be mistaken." Because if he wasn't, then I'd made a mistake. A terrible, terrible mistake.

Adam's blue eyes filled with compassion. "I'm sorry, Alexa. You have no idea how much I wish I was wrong. But the ME has made a positive ID."

"H-how?"

He ran a hand through his tawny hair, leaving it standing on end. "It looks to be by the same method as the Changs and Hawkins family, according to the officers on-site."

I shook my head in denial. "That's not possible. The Shade was here the whole time." I felt a slow, sliding numbness creep into my body. It pulled me toward the earth, beaconing me to lie down. "It came after Gloria."

"Apparently it wasn't here the whole time," he said.

It had killed him first, then had come here. I tried to swallow and ended up choking instead. "Stephen promised that he'd stay out of the Hawkins's house."

"He did," Adam said.

How had I miscalculated the pattern? "If he wasn't at the Hawkins's house, where did they find him?" I could have sworn the pattern was seven-six-seven, the same number sequence the Shade had called itself when communicating with me on the Talking board. I'd counted the client list myself multiple times to be sure I hadn't miscalculated. And now my little math error had cost Stephen his life.

"His friend on the crime scene cleanup crew gave him access to the Changs' residence. He had his investigative equipment with him, set up throughout the house. It appears he was trying to contact the spirits of the newly departed."

I'd been so focused on stopping the Shade that I'd forgotten about the demons. The little bastards kept popping up like a twisted game of whack-a-mole.

"It's all my fault. I wouldn't let the Paranormal Friends Society follow me. They told me they wanted in on the investigation and I told them no. I thought I was protecting them. But I can't protect anyone. Not without being able to see what I'm fighting. It's like battling blind." I balled my fists and kicked the side of my truck with my steel-toed boot. Pain shot up my leg.

"Seeing your opponent doesn't make you invincible. Sometimes all it does is remind you how fragile life can be," Adam murmured.

I rubbed my foot. "I know you're trying to make me feel better. And I really appreciate it. But it's not going to work this time. Stephen's dead. There might not have been any love lost between us, but I didn't want him dead." Crap in one hand, Alexa, and wish in the other. See which one fills up faster.

"I have a question for you and I need you to give me an honest answer," Adam said.

I could feel the energy drain from my body. I was tired of hunting this Shade. I was tired of the thing hunting me. I was sick of demons springing up like jack-in-the-boxes around every piece of furniture.

Adam paused, watching me. Waiting for I don't know what to happen.

I couldn't go on like this. The odds were stacked against me. There had to be a way to defeat them. I'd thought by getting to Gloria's on time that I'd figured out a way to thwart my enemy, but I hadn't.

Instead of fighting, I'd huddled in the corner with Gloria, rooting for a dead dog I couldn't even see. I blew out a frustrated breath.

Adam stroked his thumb over my knuckles. "How did you know the creature would be here?" he asked.

I was tired of lying. Or maybe I was just tired, period. I looked at Adam. His eyes were trained on me, practically begging me to let him in. I rolled my neck, then met his gaze. "Because it's following a sequence of numbers and working its way toward me."

"Why do you believe that?" he asked.

"Because when I first met it, I'd been playing with a Talking board. The thing introduced itself as seven-six-seven. It gave me that as its name. I didn't know at the time that not giving a name was really bad," I said. "It can only filter through my list of clients so many times before it runs out of names. After it does that, I will be the only common denominator left."

* * * * *

The drive to the Changs' home was quiet. The neighborhoods were asleep, nestled beneath a canopy of green. Smog still filled the air, but at night you couldn't really see it unless you were by bright lights. The change made the city look clean—at least until the light of day revealed its hidden scars.

We arrived at the Los Feliz crime scene on Dundee in record time. The yellow tape that had been previously removed was back up, circling palm tree trunks. A glaring reminder that death had returned for a second visit. The lights of the squad cars flashed on the walls of the mansion like a macabre child's mobile.

I took in the scene dispassionately, watching characters dressed as policemen act out their unscripted roles. I still couldn't feel anything. Not even the cold. I was afraid if I did, I'd shatter into a million little pieces and no one would be able to put me back together. Not even Adam. And despite having only known him for a few days, I knew he'd try.

We got out of the vehicle. Adam had insisted that he drive and I'd agreed. I wasn't in any shape to drive. And I certainly wouldn't be after we completed our walk around inside. We'd left my truck at Gloria's house. It would be safe there for the night.

"You ready?" Adam asked, watching me carefully.

I shook my head. "No," I said. "How could I be?"

"That's good," he said. "I'd be worried if you had said yes."

I tried to smile, but my lips weren't cooperating. We suited up into protective gear and entered the scene. I still didn't understand how Adam gained permission for me to be there. And didn't care anymore, now that all my days had started to blend into one long bloody nightmare.

The house was cold. Not even the warm bodies on the police force could take the chill away. Or maybe it was just me. I couldn't seem to feel my toes or fingers, even though Adam had just released my hand.

The entryway looked normal. No sign of blood or a struggle. The Changs' possessions had been removed, along with the grid. I glanced around at the newly painted walls. The cleaning crew had done a good job. Why was I noticing such benign crap?

I stepped into the foyer and was immediately swallowed by the dark emptiness. I noticed some of Stephen's equipment set up, infrared cameras and EVP recorders.

There still was no sign of him beyond the equipment. I couldn't even smell blood. Weird, that. Normally by now it would be spread everywhere.

The handprint on my shoulder began to burn. I rubbed my arm absently, then turned to Adam, hoping there'd been some kind of mistake and knowing that there hadn't. Why couldn't I live in denial? It was a much nicer address than my current residence on reality street.

"He's in the other room." He pointed to the bedroom.

I nodded, then followed him through the doorway. More police had gathered in a corner. I couldn't see what they were looking at.

"Where is he?" I asked.

Adam glanced at me. "He's in the bathroom, Alexa. At least what's left of him."

My heart started to thud.

Not the bathroom. I looked around half expecting to see Huli Jing's cherub face. The crowd parted as we neared. At first I couldn't see anything, then the smell hit me. A sickening combination of bile and intestine followed swiftly by blood. Lots and lots of blood. I swallowed repeatedly and began to breathe through my mouth. It didn't help. The odor still came through like a persistent mosquito, dive-bombing you in the night.

The last investigator moved aside and I got my first glimpse of what remained of my ex-boyfriend. Blood dripped from the ceiling in crimson stalactites. Chunks of what could only be described as meat, clogged the dual sinks, toilet and bathtub.

I stared, unable to differentiate one part from another. He'd been ripped into bite-sized pieces and scattered like chum around the room. I closed my eyes, but the vision remained. Burned into my mind as deeply as the handprint on my shoulder.

"Are you sure it's human?" I asked.

"They found his wallet in the tub. It was all that was left

of the poor bastard," Adam said.

My mind refused to acknowledge what my eyes were telling it. The carnage was too much to process.

"There's something else you need to see, Alexa."

How could there be anything else? Wasn't this bad enough? I forced my gaze back to what was left of the body and choked.

"We found a message on the mirror," Adam said. "It's the same one we found at the previous crime scene. This murder was personal."

I looked at him. "They all were," I whispered. I didn't have to ask what the message said because I already knew.

Adam stared at me, gauging my reaction. "It was written in Stephen's blood with one of his fingers," he continued.

I gulped hard as my stomach pitched. "Let me guess, it said, *Did you miss me.*"

He looked at me askance. "How did you know?"

I took one last look at Stephen's remains. "Because the Shade that killed my parents asked me that question seven years ago." Bitter laughter bubbled out. "The damn thing won't take no for an answer."

Someone started screaming. All eyes were upon me. The sound grew louder. Shrieks of pain. Cries of terror. Roars of frustrated anger, emanating from the depths of a wounded soul. The never-ending onslaught refused to quiet. I looked around, but couldn't figure out why the sound wouldn't stop. *Someone please make it stop.* My hands covered my ears to no avail.

Strong arms surrounded me, sweeping my feet off the ground. I was moving through the house. The uniforms blurred before my eyes. The sound continued as Adam sat down outside with me cradled in his lap.

A hand brushed through my hair. "Shh, it's all right, Alexa. It'll be okay."

The cries stuttered and I hiccupped.

Adam pulled me closer and began to rock. "Let it out.

You'll feel better if you let it all out," he murmured.

It was at that moment that I realized the screams had been coming from me. I'm not sure how long we sat there, but Adam didn't once try to pull away. Investigators came and went, but he didn't seem to notice or care. The world at that moment revolved around me and what I needed.

The clank of a gurney signaled the coroner's departure. A black bag sat on top the table, jiggling like Jell-O as it was rolled to an awaiting van. Lumpy in sections and flat in others, the bag outlined what remained of Stephen Reynolds—a gelatinous soup of human body parts.

Adam continued to soothe me as the van drove away. I didn't really want to move out of the comfort of his embrace, but I couldn't take the looks being sent my way by the other officers. Adam brushed a stray hair out of my eyes.

"Are you feeling better now?" he asked, searching my face for answers that I knew he wouldn't find.

"I'm sorry." I rubbed my eyes. "Not sure what happened in there."

Adam's knuckles skimmed my cheek, his touch gentle. Soothing. "You just found out that you've lost a friend. I'd say that's cause to be upset."

"We weren't close." I sniffled and rubbed at my face.

One side of his mouth kicked up. "In this circumstance, that doesn't matter. You used to date this man. At one time you cared for each other. You can't sweep it away and ignore your emotions, Alexa. Give yourself permission to feel the pain of grief. If not for yourself, then for Stephen."

My head rose and I met Adam's unwavering gaze. "You think I ignore my emotions?"

"That's not what I said."

"No, it's what you implied."

His grip tightened. "That's not true. I know that you feel something for these people."

My face twisted with bitterness that burned into my soul. "Something? It's more than something, Adam." I pushed off his warm lap to stand. Fury engulfed me. "I'll have you know that I've lived with this pain ever since I was thirteen years old."

Chapter Seven

The funeral was held on a green hillside, overlooking the San Fernando Valley.

All thirty members of the Paranormal Friends Society were there gathered around Finn, trying their best not to focus on the mahogany casket about to be lowered into the ground. Stephen's last foster family sat under a white tent that had been erected for the services, while a minister presided over the funeral.

The family probably thought he'd left them some money. They were in for a surprise, since the ghost-hunter society had paid for the funeral.

I parked my truck some distance away and turned off the engine. It sputtered for a minute, then died. A light breeze filled with the aroma of freshly cut grass brushed my short blonde hair. Too bad it wasn't strong enough to blow away the sadness. I clutched the rusted door for strength. It creaked under the effort.

Waiting here wouldn't change what I had to do. I left the security of the truck and plucked the yellow roses from my garden off the seat and shut the door behind me. I made my way across the headstone-covered lawn toward the small crowd.

Without the headstones, this place would be just another lush hillside perched under the California sun. As it was, light glinted off the stones like bones floating on a sea of green.

All eyes were upon me, when I leaned down out of respect for Stephen and gave my condolences to his foster mother. She wept silently into a handkerchief and looked away. Probably to keep me from noticing the lack of real tears.

Before I could address Stephen's foster father, gooseflesh tickled my back. I slowly straightened. I didn't have to look to know that the amateur ghost hunters were glaring at me, but I did anyway. I deserved their scorn and worse. The only one who wasn't tossing visual daggers my way was Finn.

His green eyes remained red-rimmed, but welcoming.

"What is she doing here? It's disrespectful." I heard someone say. "She shouldn't be here. It's her fault that Stephen's dead."

My shoulders tensed as I made my way to the coffin. What could I say? They were right. It was my fault that Stephen was dead. I tried to warn him, but I could've done more. Said more. Maybe if I had, he'd still be alive.

Tiny white bouquets of death lined the grave. I stared at the lilies and wondered what Stephen would've made of this scene. He'd never been one to appreciate flowers in life. Didn't see the need to give or receive them. Yet here he lay, ready to be put into worm-filled land and covered with dozens upon dozens of slowly fading blooms. And I was about to add to the pile.

I took off his newly repaired leather jacket and laid it on top of the coffin. It seemed more fitting there, than on my back. The black leather and silver zipper reflected the sunlight. I stared at it for a moment, running my hand over the smooth calfskin. I didn't want it anymore. It would only serve as a reminder. A reminder I didn't need. I placed the yellow roses on top of the jacket and stepped away.

The minister began wrapping up the service. I stopped listening after "though I walk." I knew what he would say. It was the same thing said at all the other funerals I'd attended this past week. The Hawkins's relatives had been polite when they'd asked me to leave. I give them credit for not running me off on sight. I'd been chasing death for so long that I didn't stop to think that it might be following me.

Anger lapped at my heels in ugly black waves, joining the hatred coming from the people surrounding the casket. I'd known most of the Paranormal Friends Society members for years, so their rejection hurt.

I could've stayed home, probably should have, but I wasn't the type to take the coward's way out. Besides, Stephen and I had dated for a while. We'd been friends even longer. My only regret was that we hadn't maintained that friendship. Now it was too late.

I stared at the glossy wood, so stark against the green. Traffic buzzed like angry hornets on the freeway below. The service had been a closed casket. No surprise there. The mortician would've had to have been Dr. Frankenstein to piece Stephen back together after the attack.

A hand brushed my fingers and I glanced down. Finn had hooked his pinky around mine. A tiny show of solidarity that did more than any words could. I squeezed back and listened to the drone of the minister's words die. Before long the service had ended and the Paranormal Friends Society group began to disperse.

Finn turned to me as he said his last good-bye. "What are you going to do now?"

"I'm going to kill the thing that took out Stephen." I shrugged. "It's the least I can do."

"How are you going to do that?" His body trembled. It took me a moment to realize it wasn't out of anger, but concern.

I gave him a small smile, then said, "Worst case, we'll

use those seals."

"Solomon's?" Finn asked.

Hooking my fingers into the front of my jean pockets, I nodded. "I can't let it get away with this."

He shook his head. "I don't like it. You're going to end up just like Stephen, if you aren't careful. What about your business? Who'll take care of Shaggy?"

I scoffed. "What business? Because of my newfound celebrity, people have stopped calling. I've even had clients phone and beg me to stay away from them. They think I'm some kind of jinx. And you know what? They're right. Pretty soon I'm going to have to use my state license and take a *real* dry-walling job."

He glanced at the ground before meeting my gaze once more. "Would that be so bad? You could do that and go back to school."

I'd thought about walking away over the years, especially when my need for the hunt got worse and I wasn't getting any closer to catching my parents' murderer. Back then I had a choice. That option died with Stephen. "No, it wouldn't be bad." I sighed. "But it also wouldn't be right."

He pushed his glasses up to sit on the bridge of his nose. "None of this is your fault, Lex. You couldn't have stopped this thing had you been there."

"You don't know that."

His sad eyes met mine. "Yes, I do," Finn said.

"I might've been able to drive it away with my EMP device."

He slowly shook his head. "Doubtful. I think it would take something a lot stronger to kill what attacked Stephen." His expression hadn't changed, but there was something about Finn's response that gave me pause. I searched his face. Finn's Adam's apple bobbed in his throat like a cork on a lake.

"Finn?" I drew his name out in a warning.

He avoided my gaze. "What?"

I stepped closer, so no one could overhear our conversation. "What aren't you telling me?"

He glanced around nervously. I didn't have to be psychic to know he was considering a lie. My eyes bore into him. Finn knew something. Something important.

"Stephen had a webcam with him the night he died. He was convinced that this case would change the face of ghost hunting. He sent me live feed for the first few hours of the investigation. I got bored and decided to step out for a sandwich. It only took forty-five minutes. When I returned, the picture had been replaced by static." He fidgeted. "I figured I'd lost the live feed. No big deal, you know? It wasn't until the next day, when I played the recording that I realized what had happened. By then, the police were already on the scene."

My stomach churned. "Finn, are you telling me that you recorded Stephen's death?" The thought of watching Stephen being ripped apart was a horrifying, but I needed to know what really happened to him.

Finn shook his head violently and grimaced. "No. God, no. Nothing like that. How could you? I can't believe the way your mind works."

I grabbed him. "My imagination has had a lot of help lately. Now spill it. What did you record?"

Finn's shoulders tensed and he suddenly looked uneasy. "Nothing."

I tightened my hold on his arm and he pulled away. "Finn, if you get any stiffer, you're going to crumble. Now tell me what happened?"

He blew out a heavy breath. "It was probably just a hoax. You know how people are always trying to interfere with our investigations," he said. "Remember that time in Long Beach at the *Queen Mary*. Can't believe they thought we'd fall for the old 'lipstick on the mirror' trick."

The logical part of Finn refused to accept what it had witnessed. It was human nature to look for a pattern or explanation in a chaotic world. I wouldn't expect any other reaction from someone with a scientific mind. But I needed to know what he'd captured, so I pushed Finn out of his comfort zone into the land of pain and loss.

Clasping his shoulder, I said, "Stephen's dead. The only way I can help him is if I have all the facts. Who did you see, Finn?" My voice lowered to a soft whisper.

"It wasn't a who," he said. An edge had crept into his voice that I'd never heard before. "It was a *what*."

I took a deep breath and let it out slowly. "Describe it."

He shook his head and strode off across the lawn. "Forget it. No way."

After a short jog, I caught up with him. "Please Finn. It's important. I need to know what you saw."

His green eyes widened. The color deepened in intensity. "Don't make me do this, Lex." He shoved his hands in his pockets.

I brushed a curl away from his face. "This isn't for me. It's for Stephen."

He swallowed audibly. "Low blow."

"I know." I'd purposely played on Finn's friendship in order to get his cooperation. I wasn't hunting the Shade just for Stephen. Although that was part of it. The real truth was that I was doing this as much for my family and me as I was for anyone else.

He took a resigned breath. "It was dark. The image wasn't clear."

"I understand. Just tell me what you could make out."

Finn looked at me with watery eyes. Pain filled the tiny lines near the corners of his eyes, causing them to appear deeper. "It didn't have a distinctive form, it was more shadowy than anything. But its eyes. I don't think I'll ever forget its eyes."

"What about them?" I could barely hear him over the blood roaring in my ears. For years I'd dreamed about this creature, wondering if I'd only imagined seeing it. Now I no longer had to wonder. Finn and Stephen, rest his soul, had somehow managed to capture it on digital.

Finn's face paled to a lovely hue of white marble. "They were blue. Not the kind of blue you get from contacts, but blue like they were frozen on the inside. The temperature readings in the room were minus fifteen Celsius. I know this sounds insane, but it's the truth."

I hugged him. I couldn't help it. He looked so lost. Like a child who'd just been told there was no Santa Claus. I pressed my lips to his ear. "It doesn't sound crazy to me."

He looked at me, his green eyes pleading. "That's not reassuring coming from you, Lex."

I laughed, even though his words stung. The last thing I wanted was to be considered insane by a paranormal investigative group. What did that say about me?

"It's okay, Finn," I reassured, tightening my embrace. "Everything is going to be okay. All I need from you is a copy of that recording."

Finn stiffened in my arms.

I pulled back. "What?"

"I erased it," he said quietly.

I couldn't have heard him correctly. There was no way Finn would do something so irresponsible. "What do you mean you erased it? You made a copy first. Right?"

His gaze dropped. "No. I didn't deem it necessary." He toed the spot where he stood.

"What!" I shouted. "Finn, how could you?" Some of the people, who'd been making their way to their cars, turned to look at us.

He shoved me away. "I don't need a lecture about ghost-hunting protocol from someone who thinks the rules apply to everyone but them."

"This has nothing to do with rules," I hissed. "Did you ever stop to think that it could've been the killer on the video?" My voice rose again before I could stop it, drawing the attention of all the remaining mourners. Even the minister paused from comforting the family to shoot me a look of condescension.

"It's gone, Alexa. I'm sorry," he said.

I watched my proof slip through my fingertips and kicked the ground hard enough to send a divot of grass flying into the air. "There's something I don't get," I said.

Finn's head was bent and his shoulders hunched in. His glasses had slipped down his nose, causing him to peer over the frames. "What's that?"

"Even if the image Stephen sent you wasn't the murderer, that recording was the proof you've been looking for. It would've put the Paranormal Friends Society on the map in the ghost-hunting community. As their leader, you would've been famous. You could've lectured around the world. Why would you blow an opportunity like that?"

Finn gave me a queer look before arching a brow.

"Okay, not you per se, but certainly your organization. People have been searching for the truth since the dawn of mankind. How could you erase irrefutable proof that something exists on the other side?"

Finn looked me dead in the eyes and lowered his voice. "Because if that's what's waiting on the other side, then I think people would rather live in ignorance. I know I would."

<h1 style="text-align: center;">CHAPTER EIGHT</h1>

I strode toward my truck with Finn in tow. There was nothing left for me to do, but return home. As disappointed as I was with his actions, I couldn't fault him. Finn had lived a relatively happy skeptical life. To confront the creature on the recording would mean reevaluating everything he ever believed to be true.

I always knew Finn was a nonbeliever. I just never understood how far he'd go to remain blissfully unaware until now.

"I know that you had good intentions, Finn. I don't blame you for wanting to pretend none of this happened." I pointed to Stephen's gravesite. "I would if I could." Our gazes met to exchange a moment of shared pain. "Here's the thing, though. You may have erased the creature on the video, but you'll never be able to erase the memory from your mind." I gently tapped the side of his head.

Finn blanched.

The Paranormal Friends Society lingered near their cars, waiting for Finn.

"I'd better go," I said.

"We're holding a memorial at the house. You're

welcome to come," he said.

"Thanks, but I don't think I'd be welcome." I left Finn standing on the lawn with only his thoughts for company. As I walked across the grass to my truck, I took care not to step on any of the headstones. I'm not superstitious, but I am cautious.

My truck had sprouted a new hood ornament while I'd attended the funeral. Gabe had his tall frame planted against it. He'd folded his duster and placed it beside him. His eyes weren't shaded from the sun, yet he didn't squint. I could see the rich brown depths clearly. He'd pulled his dark hair back into a loose queue. Black jeans hugged his long legs and his white shirt billowed gently in the breeze. The contrast between his deeply tanned skin and the fair fabric was striking. But there was something about the casual stance that seemed off, almost like it was an act.

What was he doing here? It wasn't like he knew Stephen. How did he even know about the funeral? Was he spying on me because I told him that I wouldn't back off from hunting the Shade? I dismissed the idea quickly as paranoia. Perhaps he was checking out the paranormal society, eyeing the competition. You can learn a lot about people by studying how they grieve. Somehow I doubted that was the reason.

I thought about the lost recording and the blue-eyed shadow. Even though it was warm, I shivered. In the right lighting, Gabe with his dark countenance could pass for a shadow. *Yeah, sure, Alexa.* He could disguise himself as a nearly seven-foot-tall transparent shadow. Real inconspicuous.

Frowning, I went to see what tall, dark, and dangerous wanted. Despite his broodingly handsome face, something about Gabe made me decidedly uneasy. Maybe it was his predatory gaze or his unnatural stillness. I couldn't pinpoint the exact reason. It was a lot of little things that caused the spot between my shoulder blades to twitch.

I slowed as I neared the truck to admire the walking

billboard for perfect genes. "What are you doing here?" I gave a quick glance over my shoulder to the gravesite.

He covered the distance between us, until only a few steps separated us. "Can't I honor a fallen comrade?"

"Sure, but you didn't know Stephen. So that begs the question, why would you?" For some reason I wanted to catch him in a lie. Anything to diminish that air of perfection that cloaked him. To destroy the mask so I could see what was hiding behind it. And there was no doubt in my mind that Gabe was hiding something.

Those dark eyes fell upon me, heating momentarily before he looked away. "I may not have known him." He watched the crowd absently. "That does not mean that I do not respect the job that he has done."

"What are you talking about?"

He turned back. "Stephen was a ghost hunter, was he not?"

It was my turn to feel discomfort. "Yes, but I wouldn't exactly put him in our league. All Stephen did was search for proof that the other side exists. He never vanquished. At least he didn't when I was active in the group."

He shrugged one shoulder. The graceful movement took a whole three seconds to complete. "Yet, he is the one being laid to rest, while we stand here arguing over semantics in the glorious sunshine." Despite his claim about the heat, I noticed Gabe shiver. For L.A., the temp was a little on the cool side, but it was still sixty-seven degrees. Far from cold.

"What happened to you the other day? I tried to introduce you to Adam, but when I turned around, you were gone."

His dark eyes glittered like marbles. "My apologies for the abrupt departure, but I received a message and had to depart at once," he said.

"Forgive me for being rude, but I think that's a load of horse crap. You could've stuck around long enough to meet Adam, but instead, you ran like a common criminal. Running makes cops curious. They wonder what you're hiding. Adam tried to get your plates, but you didn't have any."

Gabe's mouth canted in an amused smile as he pointedly ignored my remark about the law. "The car is new. It hasn't been registered yet. I see no need for temporary tags. You sound as if you took my sudden departure personally. By chance, did you miss me?"

I ground my teeth until my jaw hurt. Of all the questions he could've asked, it had to be that one. "I did not miss you."

His long lashes dropped to half-mast. "I believe you doth protest too much."

"Shakespeare? Really?" I moved closer, craning my neck. "Why are you here, Gabe? And don't you dare say to pay your respects. You don't give a damn about Stephen or any of this."

He grinned, an irritating display of perfect white teeth that didn't match his mocking tone. "I can't fool you, can I? We know each other too well."

I sidled back. "No, we don't. I know nothing about you other than what you've told me, which I might add, has been superficial at best. And unless you've investigated me, you don't know anything about me."

He bent down until we were staring eye to eye. "But you do know me. Don't you, Alexa?"

I started to deny his claim and realized I couldn't. We were strangers, but at the same time we weren't. I was intrigued by the connection I felt between us and frightened by it. The bond was odd. Kindred spirits—yet rivals. Deep down we were alike in more ways than I cared to admit. How was that possible, when I knew nothing about him?

My thoughts immediately jumped to Adam. As much as I cared about him, Adam would never understand the driving need that propelled me. The fever burning beneath my skin. The relentlessness that demanded that I wipe every last Shade out of existence. But somehow Gabe did. He understood it because he lived the same life. He was a hunter first and foremost.

Gabe's grin widened. "I thought as much. Birds of a feather and all that." He waved his hand in dismissal.

I looked around, but the cemetery had emptied, leaving only us, and the caretaker who'd started covering Stephen's casket with dirt. "Yeah, no one here but us chickens."

He tipped his dark head back and laughed at my cartoon reference. The sound rumbled through my body like tribal drums, causing it to respond instantly. Something wild and unfamiliar raised its snout inside of me, preparing to answer a primal call.

I took two steps back and did the one thing that has saved me on many occasions—I got angry. "I don't have time for games. I have a Shade to hunt." I stepped around him and reached for my door.

In a blink, Gabe was standing in front of me, blocking my entry into the truck. I collided with his hard male chest. Strong hands shot out and gripped my arms to keep me from falling, or maybe he'd thought I was going to run away. Heat spread from his cool fingertips, through my long-sleeved shirt, straight into my skin.

I tried to jerk free, but Gabe refused to release me. Instead, I found myself folded into his arms. I struggled harder.

"What are you doing? Let me go," I demanded, as emotions warred inside of me. "I don't need to be comforted by you."

"Shh," he murmured, his lips pressing dangerously close to my ear. "I'm not the one doing the comforting."

I stopped struggling, unsure how to respond to that admission. Was he serious? Or was it a diversionary tactic to get me to calm down? Either way it worked.

He continued to rock from side to side. "Do not worry, I will release you in a moment." His palm skimmed the length of my spine, brushing the bare skin peeking out at my waist. "You are softer than I imagined. Your flesh feels like down under my fingertips. And it's surprisingly warm. I didn't expect that. You are very fortunate indeed to have inherited such a thing."

Okay, that wasn't creepy at all. "Gabe, I'm not going to ask you again. Let me go," I said a tad breathlessly.

He let out a soft chuckle. "I give you my word that you have nothing to fear from me on this day. I came here to warn you, little Gosling."

I stilled. Every muscle in my body locked as I ran the odds of the use of that word being a coincidence. Not even Vegas would take that bet. "What did you just call me?"

I'd heard that term before. First with Huli Jing, then the afternoon I ran into Ryan Hawkins at the Gonzalez residence. Both had come from the mouths of demons. Demons masquerading as little kids. Gabe was no kid, but it couldn't be a coincidence that he'd used that word.

His hands stopped their soothing motions on my spine. "It is unimportant. I will call you Alexa if that is what you'd prefer. What is important is that I believe the prey we seek may be coming after you."

"Let him come. I'll be ready." My fingers moved of their own accord to the front of his soft cotton shirt, causing my hands to tingle. I refused to acknowledge the steely cold strength hiding beneath the material. I flattened my palms and shoved with all my might.

Gabe tipped back on his heels and fell into the door of my pickup truck. The movement caused him to release me in order to catch himself. It wasn't long, but it was long enough for me to escape.

He brushed at his shirt. "That was entirely unnecessary."

This man *was* dangerous. I couldn't allow myself to forget that again. "Maybe to you, but not to me."

"All you had to do was ask me and I would've released you," he said, annoyance clear in his voice.

"I believe I tried that first, but it didn't work. Now I'm going to ask you again, why did you call me gosling?"

"Because you remind me of a featherless baby bird that does nothing, but chirp, chirp, chirp because it cannot fly," he said.

I knew he'd just insulted me, even if I didn't understand how. "I'm going to leave now," I said. "I'd appreciate it if you'd step aside."

A look of incredulity crossed his features. "What, no thank-you?"

I tilted my head and conjured up the most mocking tone I could muster. "Thank you for the four-one-one, Gabe. But here's a bulletin for you, I already knew that the Shade was after me."

"Shade?" His frown eased. "Ah, I understand now. That is your term for the walking dead. Interesting. Well then consider this a courtesy call, while paying my respects of course." He moved out of my way.

I pulled the door of the truck open and climbed in. "I'm curious. Since when have you become such a sharer of information? The last time we spoke you said that you worked alone and planned on catching the Shade without me. Doesn't warning me defeat the purpose?"

He ducked his head into the vehicle until our lips were mere inches apart. His cool breath fanned out over my warm cheeks, forcing me to breathe in his exhalation. My jaw clenched and I leaned back a couple of inches to add distance between us, while my eyes involuntarily locked on his mouth.

"You are such a fascinating creature," he said, studying my face. "I've never met anyone quite like you." He inhaled. "Your scent is even different than the others. Richer. Sweeter. Dare I say, *succulent*."

My eyes narrowed. "Are you trying to seduce me?"

He cocked his head and considered my question. "I haven't decided yet."

My breath left in a rush. I couldn't seem to produce enough spit to swallow properly. My tongue darted out to moisten my lips.

Gabe caught the movement and his nostrils flared, but otherwise he didn't react. His eyes captured mine, swirling spirals of chocolate quicksand, designed to trap and devour prey.

He leaned closer. There was nowhere for me to go. He was going to kiss me. At the last second, he changed course. I wasn't disappointed. *Really.*

His lips trailed along my cheekbone until he reached my ear. There he pressed forward so that I could *feel* every syllable uttered from his sensual mouth. "Alexa, can you hear me?"

I nodded and closed my eyes. My body quivered as his lips brushed my lobe. I had to bite my tongue to keep from groaning aloud.

"The only reason I'm sharing information now is because I've decided to use you as my bait. And what lovely bait you are," he said with a flick of his cool tongue. My insides melted. "I doubt the rogue will be able to resist. I know I'm finding it difficult to do so."

His words finally registered in my befuddled mind. I should've known he hadn't warned me out of the goodness of his heart. You had to have a heart in order to do that. And Gabe was clearly without. "You're such a saint," I snapped, jerking my head away.

Gabe's lips twitched. "Close," he said, then left without another word.

* * * * *

Frustrated and antsy, I drove to the beach. I wanted to be alone before heading back home. I knew Adam would be waiting to see how the funeral went and I didn't feel like talking about it. I also wanted to think about Gabriel's warning. I refused to contemplate the rest of our conversation.

Using myself as bait wasn't a half bad idea. I knew this thing was after me. Why not make it easy on it and save a few lives in the process? Of course, that still left the teeny tiny problem of how to destroy it.

It was far stronger than anything I'd ever encountered. I didn't think the pop divas or the EMP were up to the job. I wasn't sure anything would be. How do you fight what you can't see?

The question rolled around my head like a marble circling an endless drain. Finn had mentioned Solomon's Seals. I had found them on the Internet, mainly in the form of trinkets sold at New Age sites. Would the symbols really work or had they been bastardized to the point of uselessness? I didn't believe in magic and mumbo jumbo. But I was quickly running out of options.

The waves rolled in, lapping and cresting as the sun set on the horizon. The muted roar of the ocean lulled my senses and allowed me to relax, if only for a moment. I dug my feet deeper into the sand, feeling the warm granules snuggle between my toes, while the crisp salt spray bathed my face. There was nothing like a visit to the ocean to make you realize how small you were and how little your problems mattered in the scheme of things.

I got up before I started to wax poetic and drove back to the house too exhausted to think. Shaggy greeted me at the door, doing the doggy version of the potty dance. I let him out into the backyard and grabbed a frozen dinner to heat.

Despite Gabe's method of delivery, I did take his warning seriously. I'd already figured it out for myself. The Shade was coming after me. I just didn't know when. I had no intention of letting Gabe use me so that he could catch the thing I'd been after for seven years, but that didn't mean that I was stupid enough not to take safety precautions. I broke out my equipment and placed the infrared cameras and motion detector alarms around the house.

It wouldn't stop a killer Shade, but at least I'd have a little warning before it attacked. I'd worry about Huli Jing and her demon posse later. So far, they hadn't wandered far from the crime scenes. Maybe they couldn't? Or maybe that was just wishful thinking on my part.

I finished eating, then fed Shaggy. He was now napping at the foot of the bed, waiting for me to come in for the night. "I'll be there in a minute, boy. I have to do something first."

His tail wagged. I took that as an okay, then went about rewiring my house for ghost patrol. My defenses needed to be much stronger. I plugged in the last receiver and was about to go run myself a bath, when the alarm on my infrared camera went off. Goose bumps rose on my arms as I picked up my electromagnetic field detector. I swung the gauge wide and inched my way to the pop divas, but stopped short of putting the music on.

The readings were faint, which was odd since they'd obviously been strong enough initially to set my machine off. I frowned and took a step forward, abandoning my boom box until I could figure out where the disturbance was coming from. Shaggy began to howl because the siren was hurting his ears.

"I'm sorry, buddy."

I turned off the alarm and began a slow sweep. My heart rattled around in my chest, making it hard to breathe. The readings grew stronger as I neared the wall, but still remained relatively low. I shook the EMF device, but the numbers didn't change. This didn't make any sense—unless the signal was coming from outside. But that was impossible.

Without thought I grabbed my jacket and the infrared camera, and took the EMF with me. I needed to be able to *see* what was going on, but I wasn't about to go out unarmed. I tucked my electronic scrambler into my pocket and slipped out the front door.

The signal on the EMF device increased. I followed the needle across the yard, until I found myself standing on

Adam's property line. My frown deepened. I put the EMF away and lifted the camera, pointing the lens at his house. The screen momentarily flared, then shapes began to take the form of bodies. Lots and lots of bodies. I glanced up, but couldn't see anything.

I looked back at the tiny screen. The picture had changed. Now there were even more Shades surrounding Adam's house. They weren't getting inside, but that didn't stop them from trying. Repeatedly. They pressed forward, avoiding the bar-covered windows and the plant-strewn roof.

A wave of ectoplasm followed in their wake, coating the walls until it dripped down like thick snotty rain onto the grass. I almost missed the circle of salt sprinkled around the home's foundation. What did Adam need protection from? I didn't think it was snails. The sodium ring held for now, but was starting to erode due to buildup of ectoplasm. I wasn't sure how much more supernatural bombardment Adam's house could take.

What did they want? Were they after him or something inside his house?

I caught a glimpse of Adam, peeking out from the blinds, his eyes wide with terror. My hands began to shake and I dropped the camera. The scrambler wouldn't work well against outside entities. Most would escape without too much harm coming to them, but not all. I pressed the "on" button. I had to do something to drive them away and save Adam.

Screams filled the air, tearing at the night sky.

A wave of power washed over me as the first Shades exploded. Their dying energy filled my lungs and sharpened my senses, until I could smell every blade of grass, every petal on a rose. My skin electrified, causing the hair on my body to rise. Oh how I needed this.

I hit the button again, exterminating even more entities. My body jolted orgasmically as I gloried in the sound of their cries—feeling refreshed for the first time in days. Like a burn patient who'd just discovered the power of a morphine drip, I held down the button, rocking forward onto my toes.

There were more howls of pain followed by another rush. A smile crept to my lips. It burst free into a full-blown grin. I could do this all night. I glanced at Adam's house and saw the front porch light blink to life. A second later, he stepped outside.

"Alexa, what are you doing?" He looked shell-shocked as he glanced around his yard.

I was so drunk and euphoric from the energy pouring through me that I couldn't recall why I'd left my house. A beep sounded inside my pocket. I reached in and pulled out the electromagnetic field detector. The lights lit up and my sense of urgency returned. The dead were still here. Surrounding us. Surrounding Adam.

"I'm here to save you," I trumpeted, then charged forward through the fading ectoplasm and cold silence of death.

Chapter Nine

My skin tingled from the excess power crackling through my central nervous system as I ran through the residual sludge of the dying spirits. The ectoplasm clung to my pores, clogging my nostrils with its burnt sugar taint. Not even the rank odor could dispel my euphoria.

Adam's door stood open as he walked to the edge of the porch.

"Get back inside," I cried. "It's not safe." I swung my EMF around wildly, searching for the enemy as my starving senses fed voraciously.

Adam didn't move. His skin was deathly pale and he shook as his eyes tried to focus on the scene before him. "Alexa, what have you done?" he asked, then collapsed to his knees, clutching his head.

I stumbled forward on wobbly legs and reached for him.

"No. Stay back." He knocked my hand away and crumpled in on himself. Pain filled his eyes. "Why? Why would you do such a thing?"

Why? What kind of question was that? Wasn't it obvious?

I suddenly recalled all the times Adam had acted odd,

pretended to be on the phone, or reacted to things that weren't there. It all made sense now. He wasn't reacting to imaginary things. He could see them. He'd been able to see Shades this whole time, which meant, he could see what I'd done and he wasn't happy about it.

"The Shades had your whole house surrounded. I've never seen anything like it. They were after you. I had to do something," I said. "You were under attack." Not the whole truth, but close enough.

"It's my fault," he murmured.

My forehead crinkled because he wasn't making sense. "What are you talking about?"

Adam shook his head.

I tried to touch his brow, but he flinched away. "Are you sure that you're okay?"

He rubbed at his temples, tracing small circles from his forehead to his cheekbone. "I'll be fine. Just give me a minute." His face was still pale, but color had started to return.

My gaze darted to his door. "I think some might have gotten through and into your home. I can grab the camera and have a quick look around, if you like." I moved to retrieve the camera.

Adam's hands dropped away from his head and he clutched my arm, stopping me. "That won't be necessary. I think you've done enough damage for one night."

Damage? I lifted my arm out of his grip and stared at him. "I don't think you understand. Your house might be infested."

His brows drew down over his stormy blue eyes. "Do you hear what you're saying? Infested? I don't have roaches or termites. You're talking about ghosts. Spirits of people who've crossed over. People like you who used to be alive."

My muscles tensed. "The key words in that last sentence are 'used to be.' They aren't anything like us anymore. I don't understand why you have a problem with me cleansing your home. It would only take five minutes. I wouldn't even charge you for it."

"Has it ever occurred to you that I might not want my house cleansed?" Adam watched me closely, like he didn't trust me.

It was unfathomable. Why would someone want to live in a structure with Shades? "No," I said. "Most sane people want to stay as far away from ghosts as possible."

He laughed. "So now you think I'm insane? That's rich coming from someone in your line of work." His hand swept the air in front of me to indicate my appearance. "Look at you."

I sniffed loudly, brushing my short bleached blond hair with quivering fingertips, then pulled the front of my T-shirt down, until it fell to the top of my thighs. I ran my tongue over my teeth. They felt oddly fuzzy. My moist palms itched, so I dug my nails into them before scrubbing at the front of my pants in an attempt to remove nonexistent dirt.

"What about me?" I twitched, unable to stand still.

"You're an addict. Your skin is flushed. Your breathing is labored. Hell, even your pupils are dilated," he said. "If a patrolman saw you out on the street right now, he'd think you were a junkie. And he'd be right. I wish you could see yourself."

My nose took that moment to redefine postnasal drip. I sniffed repeatedly, then gave up and used my sleeve. Not very ladylike, but necessary. I didn't want to see myself right now. I had a strong suspicion that it would confirm Adam's observations.

So what if I was feeling a little thrill from the hunt. It had been weeks since my last eviction. For an adrenaline-junky hunter, that was an eternity. I didn't expect him to understand. Besides, it was perfectly natural, considering what I'd been through. If my heart pounded a smidge harder than normal, it was only because I'd been so frightened for Adam's safety. It had nothing to do with the rush of power that came from killing Shades. Nothing.

The lie slipped easily into my mind as fire ants marched beneath my skin. My body jerked and jittered. Perhaps I had felt more of a rush than usual, but that was only because I'd been dealing with more spirits than I was used to dispatching. My palms continued to itch. I scratched at them until welts rose on my skin.

I wasn't a junkie. I wasn't, damn it. My body twitched and spasmed. Adam was wrong. I took a step back. "Next time you are in trouble, you can save yourself," I said, then stomped across the yard to my house, more angry at myself than at him.

Adam let out a long sigh. "I was never in trouble," he murmured, but I heard him all the same.

I refused to look back. I couldn't bear to see the disappointment on his face. There was a soft click, then I heard Adam's door close. I was halfway across the yard, when I sensed eyes upon me. I casually glanced around. Parked down the street on the opposite side of the road, I saw Gabe leaning against his Porsche.

He was under a heavily branched elm, his dark gaze taking in my every move. Even in the fading gray light, I could see a soft glow to his eyes. You'd think that would be comforting. It wasn't. I got the distinct impression that I'd gone from bait to prey.

Gabe's face, a mask of cold beauty held the kind of expression that freezes your heart right before it plucks the beating muscle out of your chest. I shivered under his regard and judged the distance to my front door.

How long had he been standing there without me noticing? He made no move to come closer. In fact, the longer I stared, the more I realized that Gabe hadn't moved at all. He stood frozen under that tree, watching. Waiting.

For what, I did not know.

I debated whether to go see what he wanted, but I was beginning to come down from the encounter with the Shades and needed to rest. I gave him a slight wave, which wasn't returned. My middle finger shot up. I thought I saw him smirk, but didn't stick around to confirm my suspicions.

I quickly gathered my equipment, then opened the door to my house. The camera lens was covered in dirt and would need a good cleaning before I could use it again. Shaggy greeted me with soft barks and a wet nose. I closed the door behind me and locked it.

"It looks like it is just you and me, buddy." I gave Shaggy a scratch down the length of his body. His tail thumped wildly. Turning off the lights in the living room, I peeked out the blinds to see if the hunter was still there.

Gabe continued to stand sentinel, but he'd moved. His attention was now directed at my house. I thought about calling the police and having him arrested for loitering. They'd realize Adam lived on this street and would probably call him first. I might be mad about the things Adam had said, but he was in no condition to confront Gabe tonight.

Despite the distance separating us, our gazes met and held. There was no way he should've been able to see me in the dark, but somehow he did. Gabe smiled and nodded his head right before I snapped the blinds shut. He could stay out there all night for all I cared. It wouldn't get him any closer to the Shade that was stalking my clients.

* * * * *

An hour crept by, but I couldn't stop pacing. It felt as if I'd spent a week trapped inside a coffeehouse without food. My hands tingled as I ran them along my legs. No matter what Adam said, I wasn't addicted to killing Shades. It was my job. My calling. My life. Shaggy sat on the couch, watching me with his ears perked.

Stray energy crackled in my veins, causing my legs to quiver. I rolled my head and listened to the bones in my neck rattle my spine. I was not an addict. My hands shook as I scrubbed at my arms to ward off an imaginary chill. The brand on my shoulder had been fine until this episode. Now it was burning like fire. What did that mean? Did it mean anything?

"I can stop anytime I want," I said to Shaggy. He tilted his head, listening. "I can. There's nothing wrong with being good at your job. Adam doesn't know everything."

Shaggy's tail swept the back of the couch like a fluffy feather duster.

"I try to save the guy and look at the thanks I get." I shook my head. "I should've let the Shades take him out. Would've served him right."

Shaggy woofed.

I patted his head and glanced at my watch. It was getting late, but I was too hyped up to sleep. It's just adrenaline, I told myself, while I shook out my limbs. Except I'd never felt adrenaline like this—not even the night my parents were killed.

Another minute passed. I wondered if it was too late to call Finn. He might be up. We could talk theories. Maybe come up with a plan. He could tell me more about Solomon's Seals. Dismissing the idea, I let Shaggy out into the backyard to run while I jumped in the shower. Forty minutes later the water had cooled, but I was nowhere nearer to feeling like my old self.

It had always taken awhile to come down from a job. But instead of getting longer, the time between the rush and the need had grown shorter, while my cravings had gotten stronger.

How long had I been experiencing this? Two years? Three, maybe? I couldn't recall. Fire burned my insides, doubling me over. It had never been this bad. Maybe it was due to the amount of Shades I'd gone after tonight. It had been like shooting proverbial fish in a barrel. I'd lost count after twenty.

Was I addicted to hunting Shades? I always thought my need was based on revenge and being an adrenaline junky, but what if it was something else? And if it was, what did that say about me?

By two-thirty in the morning, my head was screaming and I was no closer to an answer. I tossed on blue jeans and a long-sleeved black T-shirt, then grabbed my truck keys. Shaggy scratched on the back door. I let him in and he ran for the bedroom. He looked back expectantly when he reached the doorway.

"I'm afraid you're going to have the bed all to yourself tonight, buddy," I said. "I'll be back as soon as I can."

I hesitated for a moment when I reached the front door, not sure exactly what I'd planned to do. The answers wouldn't be found here. I flipped off the lights and locked the door. A light shone in Adam's kitchen, winking out at the night. The lone beacon seemed sadly out of place in the darkness surrounding it. I guess I wasn't the only one who couldn't sleep. I thought about going over to apologize, but I wasn't sure what for. In my mind, I hadn't done anything wrong, even though he'd made me feel like it.

As much as I wanted to go knock on his door, I knew I couldn't. Adam certainly wouldn't approve of the plan that was slowly forming in my mind. I had no doubt he'd try to talk me out of it. He was cautious by nature. It was best if he remained in the dark. That way if something went wrong, he couldn't blame himself.

I sighed, then jumped in the truck and started the engine. With a groan, it sputtered to life. My eyes strayed to Adam's place. I suppose I half expected to see him come rushing out. He didn't. Disappointment hit me in the solar-plexus. It was followed by a wave of sadness. Guess his days of watching me were over.

* * * * *

Fifteen minutes later, I stood outside Finn's house, banging on his dead-bolted door. Finn opened the metal screen, rubbing sleep out of his eyes. He was shirtless, his body covered only by a pair of ratty gray sweatpants. A thin layer of curly brown hair started at his breastbone and shot straight down over his ripped stomach into his waistband. The hair on his head was smashed on one side and he hadn't bothered to retrieve his glasses. He looked utterly adorable in a sleep-deprived way.

He squinted owlishly. "Alexa, is that you?"

"Yes, it's me. Are you alone?" It didn't occur to me until this moment that Finn might have female company. I'd never really thought of him in that way, but after seeing him half-naked, I could understand how some people might. My eyes strayed back to his chest. He rubbed the hard plane absently. I felt my face heat.

"Would it matter if I said no?" he asked.

"No," I said, honestly.

Seemingly oblivious to my reaction, Finn yawned, then asked, "What time is it?"

I glanced at my watch. "Two fifty."

He blinked. "In the afternoon or morning?"

I glanced over my shoulder into the inky blackness. "You really are blind without your glasses."

Finn scowled. Ignoring personal boundaries, he leaned in close and squinted. "Geez, Lex, you look strung out. Have you been drinking?"

I flinched as the truth struck home. "No."

He stretched, his sinewy muscles rippling beneath his pale skin. When I didn't explain further, he asked, "What's so important that it couldn't wait until morning? The *real* morning, not the pretend middle of the night one."

"Let me in and I'll tell you."

He glanced over his shoulder. "Keep your voice down. Mom's sleeping."

Given her habit of taking tranquilizers to help her sleep, I didn't think anything I said or did would wake her, so I shoved my way past him. "I need you to show me how those symbols work in that book, but first put on a shirt."

He arched a brow, then shut the door. "What book?" Finn grabbed a white T-shirt that had been tossed over the back of the duct-taped recliner in his living room.

"Solomon's Seals."

Finn's eyes widened and he came awake in an instant. "Lex, I was only kidding when I mentioned those symbols. You don't want to use those. There were warnings written all over the margins."

I shot Finn a look. Was he kidding? Nothing could be more dangerous than what we were dealing with. Stephen was dead. The Changs were dead. So were the Gonzalez and the Hawkins families. How many more people had to die before someone stopped this thing?

"I think we're way past worrying about the dangers, Finn. I have to stop this Shade before it goes after more of my clients—or worse, comes after you, Adam, and the rest of the Paranormal Friends Society."

I thought about Gabe lying in wait. I hadn't seen him when I left. If he was still keeping an eye on me, he might've followed. I went back to Finn's front room, pulled the curtains aside, and peeked out. The street looked clear, but that didn't necessarily mean anything. If Gabe was as good as he claimed, then I wouldn't see him unless he wanted me to.

"What are you looking for?" Finn asked.

"An unwanted pest," I snapped.

Finn held up his hands in defense.

"Sorry, didn't mean to bite your head off." I smoothed out my shirt, worrying my sleeves. "It's been a long night and I'm not feeling very well."

Finn touched my arm. "What about Huli Jing?"

I yanked the curtains closed. "Let's solve one problem at a time."

Puzzled, he said, "I thought you said that she killed the Changs."

I threw my arms up in the air in frustration. "I'm not sure of anything anymore. Two demons had a chance to kill me, and neither one took it. Instead, they kicked my ass. That had me asking myself why? Maybe they are lackeys and can't do anything without the Shade's permission. Or maybe that wasn't what they were doing inside the homes. I don't know. I don't know enough about them to make an informed decision. I've been able to find very little on the Internet and at the library."

Finn's expression softened. "Come into the den and relax. Don't worry, I'll help. But I want to say right up front that I do so under protest."

"Duly noted." I grinned. "Now how do we get started?"

CHAPTER TEN

"We're going to have to create a magic circle in order to perform Solomonic magical rites."

"A magic circle?" I couldn't keep the skepticism out of my voice. "Are you sure you know what you're doing, Finn?"

He grumbled something that sounded suspiciously like "Do it yourself if you don't believe me," then ambled to his den. I followed, noticing that the magazines were still toppled where Adam had bumped them. The fact that Finn's mom hadn't restacked them spoke volumes about her current condition.

"How's your mom?"

"She's having a bad week." Finn's pained expression told me it was really bad.

"Maybe it's time to look into getting her professional help," I suggested.

Finn sighed. "She's seen plenty of doctors. All they do is prescribe more drugs."

There were a lot of good medical professionals out there and there were a lot who couldn't be bothered treating patients, so they just prescribed pills.

"Sorry, Finn." I squeezed his arm.

"Me too," he said, looking downcast.

"What else do we need besides the 'magic' circle?" I asked to change the subject.

Finn picked up his glasses and began to move furniture off to the side to clear a spot on the floor. "This isn't going to work if you don't believe. Intention is the power behind magic. If you're not focused, the magic will fail."

"Fine, I'll believe," I said.

Finn's expression grew serious. "You'd better, Lex. For your sake, you had better."

All the magic workers I'd ever encountered were out to sell suckers magic beans. What I lacked in belief, I more than made up for in intention. And it was my intention to kill the Shade and take out the demons while I was at it.

There was a faint stain on the floor where the table had stood. It appeared to have several points, but I couldn't make out the details other than that the pattern didn't match up with the table legs. For as long as I could remember, Finn had placed his table in the same spot. Nothing else had ever been there. At least not while I was around. A glance around the room didn't solve the mystery.

I watched Finn gather items from drawers like he was on a metaphysical shopping spree. Where had he gotten all this stuff? And why did he have it?

When his hands were full, he returned to the big table that served as a workbench. He laid the items out for me to see. There were two different kinds of chalk, white and black. A wand. A crystal. An urn. Some kind of scented oil, sandalwood, I think, and couple of plain white candles.

"Is that all we need?" I stared at the items dubiously. I couldn't imagine that these would get the result we were after, but I was desperate enough to try anything.

"No," he said. "I need you to grab some black candles out of that drawer." He pointed to a spot behind me. I opened the first one and found a Superman costume neatly folded inside, next to a purple cape.

"Finn." I bypassed the cape and held up the costume. "We need to talk."

He blushed, his cheeks crimson in the dim light. "That's for Halloween."

My brow arched. "I've never seen you wear this and we've gone to the same parties every Halloween for the past two years." I grinned. "Time to fess up."

He pointed to the drawer. "Just put it back the way you found it and get the candles."

I shoved the costume into the drawer and slammed it shut, then kept searching. Two drawers later, I found the black candles. "Got them."

I held the candles up to give them a closer inspection. There was nothing special about them beyond the flat matte color. I leaned in and sniffed. An odor of wax filled my nostrils. They hadn't even been anointed in oil. I'd read somewhere that in order to be used in magic rituals, candles needed to be anointed. Maybe that would take place as part of preparing the circle. I knew it didn't have anything to do with hunting ghosts, which begged the question...

"Hey Finn, why do you have all this stuff?"

His shoulders tensed. "Research," he said through lips so tight that I could barely make out the word.

I suspected that Finn was hiding more than the Superman costume. I passed the candles over. "Do you have anything you'd like to tell me?"

"No," he said matter-of-factly.

"Okay, then."

Finn gathered the items and opened the book. "This can't be done quickly. It's going to take some time. The circle has to be correct, along with the symbols surrounding it. I also have to etch words and symbols onto the wand and the candles. Then it'll be time to read the incantation and invoke the seal. Like I said, it's going to take awhile."

I looked at the book. "I thought we were going to use

more than one seal."

His head shot up. "No. Definitely not. It's too dangerous," Finn said. "It would be like trying to defuse different types of bombs at the same time."

"Are you saying this could blow up?" I started to second-guess my decision.

"Yes," Finn said. "If it's not done in the correct order with the correct symbols."

"That brings me back to my first question. How do you know so much about *majick*?"

"I don't—know a lot about the Solomonic rituals." Finn tapped the seals. "But I have a passing knowledge of high magic. Enough to recognize it when I see it. High magic is tricky and can be dangerous if used improperly. It's best to keep it simple, which is why we're going to start with the First Pentacle of the Moon. It'll allow you to see what has been hidden. Or at least it should. It might not work."

I wondered how long Finn had been studying *majick*. There was a difference between the kind of magic that required a hat and a rabbit and the kind that required spells. The latter kind of *majick* wasn't the kind of subject you could become an expert on after reading a book or two. It took *years* of study, years of practice before you could cast consistently.

There was nothing simple about what we were attempting. I considered arguing that it was just as easy to use two symbols, but *majick* wasn't my forte. If Finn thought using two seals at once was bad, then I'd have to take his word for it.

"What do you want me to do first?"

Finn smirked. "I suppose it would be too much to ask for you to just be quiet and allow me to work."

"Yep." I grinned. "Now give me something to do. I'm going crazy here."

By the time I got back from the coffee run, Finn had drawn two large circles, one inside the other. There were four hexagrams cradled between the two circles. Black and white candles flickered beside them, positioned north, east, south, and west. The tantalizingly exotic aroma of the oil filtered through the room. The scent teased my nose, but did little to sooth my nerves.

Several other symbols were drawn in the outer ring, along with a couple of words that I couldn't pronounce. The one word I could pronounce, *Adonai,* meant nothing to me. Finn saw me looking at it.

"It's one of God's names," he said.

I placed his caramel latte with no foam and a shot of espresso onto the table, then dug into my bagel and black coffee. Another hour passed and the sky began to lighten.

"Does it matter if it's dark?" I asked.

In all the movies I'd ever seen, people did their conjuring at midnight or at the hour of the dead, which could be two or three in the morning, depending on who you asked. My nerves were already frayed. There was no way I could wait all day. The odds of Adam finding us before we could finish went up exponentially the longer we delayed the ceremony.

Finn concentrated as he recreated some of the same symbols from the floor for the wand. "I don't think so," he said.

My stomach gurgled. "You don't *think* so. You're not inspiring a lot of confidence, Finn."

"Do you want me to finish this or not?" he asked, finally looking up.

"Sorry, please continue." I took a drink of coffee. The hot tang nipped at my tongue, shocking my taste buds, but my brain was still sluggish from lack of sleep.

"If you're worried about it," he used the chalk in his hand to point to the windows, "then close the blinds."

I hopped off the stool and shut the blinds. It just didn't seem right to do this during the day. "How long will it take once everything is ready?"

"Not long." Finn pursed his lips and scratched his head.

"At least it shouldn't. I've never actually done one of these before, but the instructions are pretty clear."

My eyes bugged. "You're following a manual?"

"Magic isn't made up out of thin air, Lex." He stopped what he was doing and turned to face me. "Would you rather I winged it?"

I thought a minute. "No, I suppose not."

"We should be ready to go in twenty minutes." He picked up his coffee and took a sip. The muscles in his arm flexed, giving me a tantalizing view of the biceps I'd seen earlier. I found my eyes drawn again and again to his covered chest, remembering what it looked like bare. I wasn't particularly happy about the fact that I couldn't strike the image from my mind. Even though we were only three years apart in age, Finn had always been like an older brother to me. Sorta cute, but untouchable. The fact that I was seeing him in a new light meant something was definitely wrong with me.

"This stuff is good. Thanks for picking it up," he said, knocking my inappropriate thoughts on their ear.

"It seems to me that I didn't have much choice." I swirled my coffee, wishing I had another gallon of it hooked up to my vein via IV. Maybe then my thoughts would stop straying to places they didn't belong.

Finn laughed. "No, you didn't."

I forced my eyes up until they were once again focused on his face. Our gazes met. Finn's unflappable expression changed, becoming unreadable. The tension in the room rose between us.

"I'm going to get some water," I said. "Need anything?"

"No." He shook his head, slowly allowing the moment to pass. "I'm good."

Finn continued to work steadily, but our progress seemed to crawl. The light behind the blinds was much brighter now. There was no way to pretend it was still dark. Just when I thought I'd reached my threshold for waiting, Finn smiled.

"It's done." He stared at his creation adoringly. "Are you

ready to give it a go?" His green eyes glowed like a mad scientist about to throw the switch.

I took a deep breath and stared at the strange circles on the floor. Finn had completed another smaller circle nearby that was chockablock with symbols. "What's that one for?" I asked.

"It's supposed to help with the incantations," he said. "The other one, the First Pentacle of Moon, should allow you to see what has been hidden."

"Like Shades?"

"Yes," Finn said. "And anything else that happens to exist," he muttered under his breath.

"Are you beginning to believe that there's more out there in the world than just Shades?" I asked, wondering if the video he'd erased had changed his mind.

Finn met my gaze. "I told you before, I don't want to know."

Even when confronted with irrefutable proof, some people refused to believe. Now I know how Mulder felt. What I didn't understand was how Finn could practice *majick* and ignore everything else. That took a special kind of denial.

Finn put his chalk down.

It was now or never. I eyed the circle warily.

"You don't have to do this, Lex. I can just throw salt on the whole thing, then wash it away."

I was sorely tempted to take him up on the offer. Invoking the seal had seemed like such a good idea, until I saw the *tools* that we were going to be working with. Their otherworldly meets craft-shop appearance made me doubt their validity.

Gabe had used the term other-worlders. Strange that it was the first thing that popped into my mind now. I shook my head, dismissing the thought and concentrated on what needed to be done.

I had come here to get help so that I could stop this

Shade. I couldn't allow my reservations and fears to prevent me from finishing the job. Seeing what I was up against was the first step in defeating my opponent. Hopefully it would be enough.

Squaring my shoulders I said, "I'm ready. Where do you want me?"

Finn's brow rose. "Talk about a loaded question. Do you really want an answer?"

So he *had* noticed me looking at him with newfound appreciation earlier. "Not now, Finn."

"Fine." He rolled his eyes, playfully, but his tone said there would be a later.

I was definitely inside the rabbit hole.

"Step inside the circle and whatever you do, don't step outside of it until I tell you that it's okay to do so. Understand?" he asked.

I nodded and swallowed hard, then stepped inside the circle. I didn't feel anything strange or supernatural. In fact, it felt like standing in Finn's den on any other day. This wasn't so bad, I thought. Then Finn began to chant, his voice low and hypnotic. I had expected him to be hesitant, perhaps clumsy, but he wasn't. If anything, it was as if he did this sort of thing all the time.

The temperature in the room started to drop and my teeth began to chatter. A gray haze thickened the air. I could hardly see Finn as he continued murmuring strange words that I didn't understand.

Something crackled and the sharp smell of sulfur burned my nose. I coughed, catching movement out of the corner of my eye. Something was in here with us. A shadow moving in the gray. My vision strained to cut through the haze, but I couldn't make out the shape clearly. All I knew for sure was that it wasn't Finn.

My head began to spin and I dropped, landing hard on the cold floor. Finn's warning rang out, "Don't break the circle." I scrambled to pull my limbs in tight. The swirling smoke went from gray to black and I gasped for air. I couldn't breathe. It was choking me.

Someone called my name, but I couldn't see them. Couldn't make out the voice. They sounded so far away. Was it Finn? I heard rustling and glanced at my feet. Black scorpions scurried over the toes of my shoes onto my clothes. I shook my leg, but they clung, their stingers drawing nearer to the bare skin under my pants.

I yelled for help. Or at least I think I did. Then I dug my fingernails into my arms, tucking my knees under my chin as I held on for dear life. The room started to spin. Around and around, faster and faster, until everything blurred.

Just when I was convinced that I was about to toss my coffee onto my shoes something popped, then sizzled like a live wire in search of a ground. Sparks flew but were quickly swallowed by the smoky fog.

The putrid scent of rotten eggs thickened. My eyes and mouth began to water. I didn't dare release my hold to wipe the tears away. I was too afraid that I wouldn't be able to pull myself back together.

Something snarled in the mire. Teeth snapped and a cool breath washed over my neck, dangerously close to my throat. This had to be a nightmare. A waking dream that refused to release me. Where was Finn? I shouted for him and closed my eyes tight.

Big mistake.

Symbols danced behind my eyelids in a kaleidoscope of color followed by the most horrific looking creature I'd ever seen. Burnt membrane-covered wings protruded from boney shoulder blades. Eyes, glacial blue, glowed against skin that could only be described as raw.

Its face was humanoid, *sort of*, if you could get past the receding gums filled with vicious fangs. Two toes held velociraptor-sized talons. Long, sinewy legs led to a concave stomach, which caused the rib bones to protrude obscenely. If this was what I had to look forward to battling, then I was in a world of hurt. The sight was enough to give my nightmares—nightmares.

"Stay away," I shouted, trying to make myself smaller.

It didn't seem to hear me and just kept coming.

In the distance, I heard Adam's panicked voice calling my name, but I couldn't see him. He yelled at Finn to stop the invocation. But it was too late. I knew that now. And from the sound of panic in his voice, so did Adam.

The ground beneath me began to tremble. Were we having an earthquake? I didn't get a chance to find out because in the next second the bottom dropped out from under me and I was freefalling into oblivion. I screamed. Or at least I think I screamed. The sound was swallowed so fast that I couldn't actually hear it.

Endless darkness surrounded me, devouring what was left of Alexa Dawn. What little air had been in the room was gone, absorbed by the hungry flames that were fast approaching. I was going to be burned alive, if I didn't stop my descent. I struggled, my hands searching for purchase, but there was nothing to grab onto. Nothing to hold. No one to save me.

"Help me, please," I called out into the inky oblivion.

The cry fell on deaf ears. The fire grew closer, bringing with it intense heat. Sweat beaded my skin. Soaked my clothes, leaving them pasted to my body. The flames rose as if in anticipation.

I saw another black-winged creature step out of the blazing inferno. I couldn't make out its face in the glare. Like death incarnate, it spread its arms wide and its soot-covered gossamer wings followed suit, waiting to catch me.

I tried to change course. My body flailed, fighting the inevitable. I screamed, long and loud.

The creature opened its mouth. Rows and rows of white teeth glowed bright against the orange flames. I felt its icy touch as it plucked me out of the air, and then cradled me against its coarse chest.

How could it be cool, when it was surrounded by so much heat? I looked at its face. Its blue eyes glowed with...*affection*? It began to coo. There was something familiar about its features. I forced myself to study them, but the flames licking at my skin kept breaking my concentration.

The creature stared back at me, blue orbs unblinking. A smile split its mouth. It stroked my face with a single talon and said, "Welcome home, Gosling."

Chapter Eleven

"*Nooo...*" I struggled against its hold, but couldn't seem to break free.

Strong arms enveloped me. "It's okay, Alexa. I've got you. You're safe. Open your eyes."

The voice sounded familiar, but I was afraid to comply in case the hideous creature was trying to trick me.

Adam's lips touched my forehead. "I promise it's okay," he said with understanding.

I cracked one lid. Sunlight splashed my face, temporarily blinding me. I tried to move my arms, but they were stuck. I fought harder.

"Calm down, it's only the sheet." Adam's large calloused hands stilled my movements, then he carefully peeled back the linens until I could move my limbs. "How are you feeling?" he asked, leaning over to shut the blinds so that I could see.

"Did anyone get the license plate number of the bulldozer that hit me?"

Adam laughed, a pain-filled sound that stabbed at my heart. "That good, eh?"

I blinked, then glanced around the room. The den was

gone, along with Finn and his mysterious circles. In their stead were sturdy wood furniture and an open closet full of masculine clothing. Photographs of Adam and what I presumed was his family filled frames on the wall. There was a chair that looked like it had been procured from the kitchen parked beside the bed. The room smelled rich and earthy, like the man.

I was in Adam's room. In Adam's bed. Shaggy was asleep beside me, his head resting on my thigh. There was a moist washcloth on my forehead and someone had removed my clothes before tucking me under the covers.

I couldn't have been more confused. "What happened? How long have I been here?" I knew I hadn't dreamt the whole thing. I still had a vague coffee taste in my mouth and my hair smelled like smoke.

"Don't you remember the ceremony?"

"Vaguely." I sat up with Adam's help. "I recall the beginning of it. We set up the candles. Finn drew stuff on the floor. There was something moving in the smoke. Something bad. Something went wrong with the invocation."

The lines around Adam's blue eyes looked deeper and white brackets framed his mouth. His hair was mussed and his clothes were wrinkled. Fresh cuts lined his arms. There were more than usual, which meant that he'd been really upset. I touched them gently. He drew back and quickly pulled down his sleeves.

"We aren't sure exactly what happened during the ceremony. That's why I brought you to my house. If you hadn't woken up, I was going to take you to the hospital, then I was going to arrest Finn for practicing magic without a license."

"Finn doesn't practice—" I thought about the faint design on the floor. It had been there before we got started. And what about the candles he kept on hand? It occurred to me that I had no idea what Finn was doing with all that paraphernalia.

How long had Finn been practicing *majick*? It had to have been for at least a year. I thought I knew the few friends that I had pretty well. But I was finding out that I might not know them at all.

"It wasn't his fault," I said.

"He could've killed you," Adam said.

"He could have, but he didn't." My fingers brushed my head. I wasn't sure there'd be any hair left. "The last thing I remember is sitting in the circles and then I was falling. The rest was just some kind of hellish nightmare filled with smoke, fire, and monsters. Freud would have a field day analyzing my dreams." I rubbed my bare arms as a sudden chill streaked its way down my spine. "Did you take my clothes off?"

Adam forced a grin. "Yeah, it was rough, but someone had to do it."

"Perv."

He laughed. "You didn't mind when I tried to get you naked the first time."

My brow arched in amusement. "I was conscious then."

"Good point." He nodded. "I removed them because you were sweating profusely and you kept trying to rip them off. I figured it would be better if I just undressed you. That way you couldn't ruin them or hurt yourself trying."

I bit back a smile. "So it wasn't just to see me naked?"

"That was only a secondary consideration." He winked. "Finn suggested that I strip you down in his den."

My eyes widened. "You didn't. Did you? I mean it's not like I'm super modest, but Finn has cameras everywhere. I don't want to wind up on some pay-to-peek website."

Adam shook his head. "No, I figured for now what you have under there is for my eyes only."

My brow shot back up before I could stop it. I was sorely tempted to correct him, but decided to let his assumptions slide. After all, Adam had managed to get me to his home and nurse me back from…from?

The flames and winged creature leapt into my mind before I could stop them. I shivered as I recalled its cool breath on my cheek. My hand automatically moved to my face to check the skin. I'm not really sure what I expected to find since it had only breathed on me, but that didn't stop me from looking for evidence of frostbite.

Adam pulled my hand away from my face and looked at my skin. "Are you sure that you're okay?"

"Yes, as good as I'm going to be. To be honest, I don't think the incantation worked."

"We'll see," he said solemnly. "I phoned Finn to get more information about the seal you invoked. I still can't believe that he helped you do something so stupid."

"I was desperate."

Adam shifted. "Do you have any idea how dangerous playing with supernatural things can be? You can't control this stuff, Alexa. If anything, it ends up controlling you."

I met his gaze evenly. "I'm aware of the risks."

"Then why in the hell did you do it?" he asked. "You could've died—or worse." Adam stood and began to pace across the hardwood floor. "There are some things we aren't meant to understand."

I shuddered at the "or worse" part. I wasn't sure what Adam was referring to, but I knew what could be worse in my mind. I pictured flames and the burnt-winged creature with the chilling breath.

"I didn't have much of a choice. Not sure if you noticed, but we've been on the losing side thus far. The only way to stop this Shade is to play on its home turf. I can't do that if I can't see it. I'm tired of fighting the invisible man."

Adam stopped pacing and ran a hand through his thick hair. "It's not a Shade, Alexa. I told you that. Spirits can't cause this level of damage."

The sheet slipped and I caught it, clutching it to my chest. "Well, it sure as heck isn't a demon. They've all shown up in the form of children, either by possession or manifestation. I know you haven't been able to see them, but take my word for it, the creepy little bastards have been there."

"I believe you," he said unobtrusively.

I paused, shocked. "Thank you."

He nodded. "You're welcome."

I looked at Adam for what felt like the first time. "Whatever this thing is, I have to stop it," I said. "I won't let anyone else get hurt because of me. Enough people have died. It has to end now."

Adam stared at me for the longest time, his face a caldron of turbulent emotions. The muscle in his cheek jumped. As if coming to some kind of conclusion, he released a heavy breath. "Did you know that the invocation is irreversible?" he asked quietly. So quietly that I almost didn't hear him.

Had I really believed that I'd do this ceremony and then only be able to see the Shade I'd been after? Yep, that about sums up my stupidity in a nutshell.

Finn had forgotten to mention that little tidbit before we started the ceremony, but I'd suspected as much. Not that it would've stopped me. I wondered if Finn knew. I hadn't bothered to ask. Hyped up on Shade dispersal energy, ectoplasm, and caffeine, I hadn't considered all the ramifications.

"I'll take your silence as a no," Adam said.

I shook my head. "I knew there was a chance that was the case. Are you sure that I'll be like this, whatever 'this' is, forever?"

"Yes," he said, a tinge of sadness in his voice. "Once invoked, the seal cannot be reversed." My expression must have changed dramatically because Adam added, "There is always a chance that it didn't work."

He was hoping it hadn't worked. No, he hadn't come right out and said so, but I could see it in the set of his features and the tension in his shoulders. Adam knew something that he wasn't sharing. It was beginning to be an annoying habit with him.

I sat back against the pillows. "How will we know? I mean do we need to go somewhere like the crime scenes to see? Or pick one of the haunted locations in the Los Angeles area? There are a few that are dependable, when it comes to Shade spotting. I haven't been able to clear the historical sites. It tends to perturb the caretakers. Something about losing money." I dismissed their concerns with a wave of my hand.

Adam's lips twitched in amusement. "Leaving won't be necessary. We can check right here." He pointed to the floor. "I have a surefire way to test you and you won't even have to get out of bed."

I looked at the spot he was pointing to, but didn't see anything. How could he test whether invoking one of Solomon's Seals had worked? And what kind of test did he have lying around? Whatever it turned out to be, I was sure I wasn't going to like it.

"You sound a little over prepared, like you've been expecting this all along."

"Actually, just the opposite. I prayed you never had to go through anything like I—like this. But what's done is done," he said.

I stared at Adam. He believed every word he'd said and sadly, so did I. "If I pass this so-called test, then you're telling me that there's no way I can return to normal. Not that I ever was normal. But my version of normal."

He nodded. "That's exactly what I'm saying."

Reality finally sunk in. I'd known there were risks. I'd have to deal with the consequences.

"Believe me, I wish I was wrong," he said. "But in this particular field, I know what I'm talking about."

"How do you know so much about the supernatural?" I asked.

"I've learned it out of necessity," he said.

"You don't seem the type to buy into that kind of stuff." I refused to let Adam know that he was scaring the crap out of me. How could I? In a moment of anger and panic, I'd brought this on myself. I propped the pillows beneath my shoulders. Every muscle in my body ached and I couldn't seem to stop shivering.

His blue eyes softened. "Looks are deceiving. Social outcasts aren't the only ones who read up on the subject. I've spent the past ten years of my life searching for a way to get rid of my curse," he said, matter-of-factly.

"Curse?" Adam was speaking, but it might as well have been in tongues for all the sense it made. Right now he sounded more like Finn than the cop I'd met a short time ago. "You're starting to worry me. You're not going to go all furry at the full moon, are you?"

"Hardly." Adam laughed, a painful sound that actually caused both of us to wince. "Why do you think I cut myself?"

"I—I don't know," I stammered. He'd spent so much time hiding his scars that I hadn't expected him to come right out and confess their cause.

His expression saddened. "Do you think I enjoy the pain?"

"N-no," I said, but I'd been afraid to ask after seeing the scars from an attempted suicide and subsequent cuttings. Only people unable to face severe emotions resorted to that type of behavior.

He sat closer. "Pain is the only way I can escape the curse. Even then, it only lasts a little while," he said, pleading with me to understand. "Drinking doesn't help. And dying only makes it worse."

I still had no idea what kind of curse Adam had, but I knew it had to be bad if it had driven him to try to kill himself.

When I didn't say anything, he continued. "Why do you think I was assigned to these cases? It wasn't chance, I assure you. Do you think they allow just anyone to bring a civilian into the crime scenes?"

I gulped. "No."

He probed. "So why do you think they let me?"

I'd been asking myself that question for weeks. "Seniority," I said, hopeful that was the case.

"Members of the Creep Squad don't have seniority like the regular force. Ours is based on *ability*, not years. The more powerful you are, the higher your rank."

I flinched when he used the derogatory term. It sounded so harsh coming from his mouth. I had never really thought of Adam as a member of the Creep Squad, not even when I'd implied as much to Finn. Still couldn't quite wrap my mind around the idea that he was part of that special unit. He seemed oddly normal.

Shame filled me. "I'm sorry I talked smack about the Creep Squad. I didn't mean anything by it," I said. "I didn't know."

"Don't be." He shook his head. "You wouldn't have changed, even if you had known."

I'm not perfect and don't claim to be, but I'd like to think that if I knew something would hurt Adam's feelings that I'd at least make an effort to avoid the subject.

"I was assigned to the squad because I have a 'gift' or a curse, depending on your perspective, that allows me to see and speak with the dead. It gives me pretty high 'seniority' as you call it, but I'm far from being the man in charge."

My eyes widened. "Who's in charge?"

"His name is Caleb Godfrey. He's currently working a case in Missouri."

I made a mental note to Google Caleb. "If seniority is based on your power and you're considered pretty senior because you can see and speak to the dead, then what can Caleb do?"

His lips canted. "It's rumored that he can speak with God."

I gaped. "As in the Almighty, Supreme Being, yada, yada?"

Adam chuckled. "That would be the one."

Nervous laughter came tumbling out of my mouth. "You're kidding, right?" It wasn't possible to have a hotline to God, was it?

Adam cocked his head and smiled. "Yes, I'm joking. No one knows for sure what Caleb's powers are, but it's safe to say that he can do more than I."

"So you can see Shades?" I asked, already knowing the answer. It had been confirmed the other night. I shuddered at the idea that I was now living in a world where I'd be surrounded by the visible dead. It had been scary enough when I couldn't see them.

"Yes," he said, matter-of-factly. "It started when I was a kid. I drowned and was clinically dead for a few minutes, before they revived me. I was twelve. My best friend at the time had been trying to teach me how to swim. I jumped into the pond and sank like a rock. I've never been the same since."

"I'm sorry." It seemed to be all I could say.

"Don't be. The dead are drawn to me," Adam said, nudging me out of my thoughts. "I have to monitor my emotions or what happened last night with the wave of dead surrounding my house, would occur every day."

"What caused them to come?"

He stared at me in surprise. "You really don't know, do you?" Heat infused his face.

"No."

His gaze intensified.

My eyes widened and I squeaked, "Me?"

Adam smiled. "More like thoughts of you."

"Sorry," I said, unsure how I felt about being the cause of Adam's torment.

He touched my hand. "Don't be."

"All those times at the crime scenes when I thought you were on your cell, you were actually talking to Shades?"

Adam ducked his head and looked away. "I was never on

the phone at those times, only when you heard it ring. It's easier to cover up what I'm doing, if people think I'm using a headset. Makes investigations that involve Nops run smoother."

I frowned. "Nops?"

"Normal cops," he said in lieu of explanation. "They already think I'm on the edge of self-destruction or insanity, so I try not to give them ammunition. Hence the Bluetooth headset."

My eyes drooped as exhaustion set in. This was all too much to take in.

Adam pulled the covers up to my chin. "Get some rest. I've given you a lot to think about. We'll pick the conversation up in a couple of hours, if you're feeling up to it."

I'd suspected there was more to Adam's quirks than met the eye, but I hadn't wanted to believe it. Not even when the truth was shoved in my face. Denial was more palatable, but I couldn't deny anything any longer.

Chapter Twelve

Adam made good on his promise. He'd let me sleep for a while. I was feeling much more alert and far less happy now that my mind was able to follow along.

"They really do prefer the term spirits," Adam said, trying to make light of the situation.

"Who does?"

He gave me a patient look. "What you call Shades are actually spirits."

I smirked. "Is that the politically correct term?"

Spirits? Shades? Ghosts? What was the difference? Nothing tangible, that's for sure. I didn't care what they wanted to be called. As far as I was concerned, they'd lost their right to vote when they'd crossed over.

I pictured all of the dismembered bodies and tried to imagine holding a conversation. The thought horrified me, but I needed to know. It would explain why the demon, Kayeri, was so upset. "Were you talking to the victims at the crime scenes or someone else?"

Adam's hand tightened on mine. "Normally I speak to the victims of violent crime. They have a harder time letting go of this life than others, since their lives were prematurely cut short. They tell me who hurt them. We apprehend the suspect. Case closed. That's why these cases have me baffled. The spirits I encountered in the homes weren't any of the victims. They were entities, which were just trying to help. The murder victims should've been there, but they weren't. I've never seen that before."

I thought about the crime scenes and Adam zoning out. "W-why didn't you tell me?" I'd noticed that something was off and had chosen to ignore it.

Acknowledging Adam's gift meant eventually I'd have to accept his abilities, when I knew that the way he'd been using them was wrong. Man wasn't meant to talk to the dead or hang out with them. There were some boundaries you just didn't cross. I knew I was being hypocritical, but I couldn't change the way that I felt.

He gave me a pointed stare. "Would you have believed me, if I'd told you?" he asked, already knowing the answer to that question.

I squirmed like a worm on a hook. "Yes. Maybe. I don't know. But since you never gave me the chance, I guess we'll never know."

Although it wasn't logical, Adam's omission hurt. I thought that we were at least on our way to becoming friends. I know friendship should come before intimacy, but in the real world that doesn't always happen. His deception brought home how little I knew about him. If he was hiding this big of a secret, what else did he have tucked in the back of his closet?

Adam sat back down in the chair, his hands folded neatly on his lap. "My gift's not something that I go around sharing with people, Alexa. It makes them uncomfortable. It makes *me* uncomfortable, but I cope with it because I have no choice. Besides, we'd just met and you were still a suspect in a murder investigation. You didn't trust me and I didn't trust you."

Well, there was that small fact. Adam was still a cop after

all. Creep Squad or not.

I sighed. "I imagine it does affect your relationships. Most people have a problem hanging out with dead people."

He watched me. "Actually, most people don't know that dead people are around. They can't sense them. That's why people like me are so popular. And contrary to what you might think, I'm not about to tell them differently. Let people live in ignorant bliss. It makes their lives happier."

I crossed my arms over my sheet-covered chest and considered everything he'd told me thus far. I replayed every interaction we'd had in my mind, searching for alternate meanings. "Wait a minute. Something just occurred to me. Last night when I asked to cleanse your home, you refused. There's a Shade living in here, isn't there?"

He gave me a sheepish look. "Yes," he said.

"Eww! You should've told me before you kissed me. Voyeurism might be your kink, but I don't go for being watched. That's just sick. You know that."

His face darkened. "I'm glad you think so little of me. For your information, I made Bernie and Ethyl leave, before things got heated. They had no interest in watching us. They were just looking out for me. As for kissing you, it wasn't like I planned it."

"Bernie and Ethyl? You mean to tell me there is more than one."

He nodded. "Their names are Bernie and Ethyl Finkelstein. They are the elderly couple who live with me."

I refused to think of them as anything but floating corpses. "You mean the *Shades* who live with you."

His expression pinched with impatience. "Like I said, they don't like that term. It's derogatory and disrespectful. Kind of like Creep Squad."

"I deserved that," I said. "But I didn't deserve being put on display at such a vulnerable moment. Why didn't you just let me vanquish them?" Hurt stung my chest, tightening my throat.

"Why would I do that?" he asked confused. "I just told you that they live with me."

"Because they're Shades." I knew I was shouting. I didn't like the idea that somewhere in the house a couple of voyeuristic ghosts were floating around. I pulled my knees into my chest and wrapped my arms around them.

He rubbed the scars on his wrist as if they still ached. "You are blowing this out of proportion. They're quite a nice couple once you get to know them. They kept me going at a time in my life when I didn't think I could go on." When he caught me staring, Adam dropped his hand away from his wrist and cleared his throat. "They're the ones behind Shaggy's appearance in my backyard. I'm afraid they fancy themselves as matchmakers."

A myriad of emotions filled me. "They did that? They touched my dog?"

His voice dropped. "They didn't like the fact that I was lonely. You made quite an impression, Alexa, on all of us. Ignoring you was impossible." Adam didn't look happy about the admission.

My mind raced as I thought about all the times Shaggy had gotten out. I touched his head in reassurance. They hadn't harmed him. I'd checked him over thoroughly the first time he'd escaped. I still didn't like the idea that two Shades had been messing with my life.

"How did they get past my supernatural defense system?" It shouldn't have been possible. I was very careful about my personal protection.

"You'd have to ask them," he said.

I took a calming breath and reined in my temper. "I still don't understand why you'd want to live in a house that was occupied by Shades. Just the thought gives me the willies."

"Didn't you hear a word that I said?"

I answered with a question of my own. "Do you have any idea how dangerous they can be? They like to pretend they're your friends. And just when you think that you can trust them, they kill everyone and everything that you love."

He cocked his head. "Is that what happened to you, Alexa? Is that how your parents died?" Adam asked softly.

I looked away, unable to meet his eyes. I knew the police had looked into my history, when I was arrested. I had no doubt Adam had read the report, but he hadn't mentioned my past until now. "It was a long time ago. I really don't remember." I lied.

"I'm sorry that you had to go through something so horrific as a teenager. I can't imagine what your life has been like." He touched my arm, caressing the fine hairs. "Please look at me."

I made myself meet his gaze.

"I know I'm not going to be able to convince you that Bernie and Ethyl are harmless, so instead, I'd like to ask you a question if I may."

My fingers tightened on the edge of the sheet and I pulled it up to my chin. "Go ahead."

"Has it ever occurred to you that maybe, just maybe, you've been killing the wrong things all these years?" he asked.

It hadn't occurred to me. I'd never questioned my actions, but I wasn't ready to admit that yet. "Since you're such an expert in the field, what should I have been killing?"

Adam shook his head. "I don't know. One thing I do know is that most ghosts have no intention of harming the living. They stick around because they loved life so much— or, as in Ethyl's and Bernie's case, so that they could save a life."

"Yours?" I asked.

His gaze dropped. "Yeah, mine."

My eyes flicked to his wrists of their own accord. "How did they save your life?"

Adam pulled up his sleeves and began to caress his scars. He didn't say, "Hey look at these." He didn't have to. The mottled skin spoke for itself.

"I had a difficult time accepting my 'gift'. I wanted it to stop by any means necessary, even if that meant taking my own life." He allowed the words to register. "Ethyl and Bernie were drawn to the pain that emanated from my body. If they hadn't shown up when they did and set off the fire alarms in my house, we wouldn't be having this conversation. They're good people. Dead or alive. I owe them."

I'd never heard of a Shade saving somebody. I mean there was the odd story here and there in paranormal journals where someone had been woken from a dead sleep by a loved one who'd passed on, to find that their house was on fire, but those accounts were rare.

What were the odds that I'd been hunting the wrong prey all these years? My stomach burned as I considered how many Shades I'd vanquished over the years. One hundred? Two hundred? More?

I hadn't thought for a minute that what I'd been doing was wrong. I still didn't. My conscience twinged as Adam's question battered me. At least not until now.

"So where do we go from here?" I asked, looking around the room. Nothing had changed in the last few hours. The walls were still light blue, the comforter a rich navy. I didn't see dead people hanging around in the corners. Shaggy hadn't suddenly developed the ability to speak, heaven forbid. I certainly didn't need my dog babbling like a cartoon animal.

Adam stared at me a moment, then squeezed my hand. "It's time for the test."

I sat up straighter and gripped the edge of the bed. "What do I have to do?"

"Nothing," he said.

Suddenly, the temperature in the room began to drop. Shaggy raised his head and looked around. His tail began to wag. I looked from my dog to Adam. "Am I missing something?"

The door opened slowly and an elderly Jewish couple stepped into the room. The man wore a pinstriped suit and spats over his polished black shoes. A red carnation decorated one pocket. His fedora sat cocked to one side on his head, shading his generous nose. He had dark brown eyes and a mischievous smile.

The woman beside him had her hair swept up in a forties back curl. Her hand was tucked into his elbow as if that were the most natural place for it to be. Her navy dress had wide shoulder pads and nipped in at her trim waist, giving her the appearance of an upside down triangle. Her lips were painted red to match the carnation in his lapel. The outfits seemed at odds with their sepia skin tone.

"Why are you dressed like that?" Adam asked, confusion marring his features. "Where are your regular clothes?"

"We couldn't exactly meet your lady friend, looking like schleps. Now could we?" Bernie nudged Ethyl with his elbow. "She's a real doll face. Isn't she?"

The woman tilted her chin and assessed my appearance. Even if I wasn't naked, I would've felt woefully underdressed.

"Her hair could be longer, but otherwise, she's perfect," Ethyl said. On cue, she turned and straightened Bernie's wide yellow tie.

Adam shook his head and fought to keep from laughing. "You guys are too much." He looked at me. "Alexa, I'd like you to meet Ethyl and Bernie Finkelstein."

The couple stepped forward. "It's nice to finally meet the dame who captured our Adam's attention," Ethyl said. "I'd shake your hand, but you know." She shrugged apologetically.

Bernie let out a catcall. "Bet you're hiding some nice gams under there." He nodded to the sheets.

The conversation continued around me as if I weren't in the room. It was a round robin of questions and answers that, had they not been coming from ghosts would've seemed almost normal—for the year 1942. Bernie and Ethyl suddenly stopped talking and looked at me expectantly.

I thought of all the things I might say. Should say. Could say. But when I went to speak, my mind blanked, then my eyes rolled back in my head and I promptly threw up on Bernie's spats.

Chapter Thirteen

Seeing dead people regularly was going to take some getting used to. It wasn't everyday you walked into a room and saw spirits milling around like they were waiting for a flight. It didn't help that every one of them felt the need to talk. Now I understood why Adam cut himself. Pain was the only thing that quieted the voices and made their images fade. I wasn't into pain, so I'd have to find another way to cope.

Adam was a patient teacher as he walked me through the various ways you could tune ghostly voices in or out. It was a lot like being a ham-radio operator in search of a signal. Some things broadcast in stereo, while others got lost in the crackle. None of them ever really went away.

At least I'd stopped feeling nauseous every time they spoke to me. It only happened every other time now. Adam had assured me it was only a temporary side effect caused by the shift in my perception. The colors around me seemed brighter than they were before the ceremony or maybe I was just finally paying attention.

Adam talked about when he'd first realized what was happening to him and how he'd nearly gone insane. He seemed genuinely relieved to be able to share his secrets with someone who'd understand.

I couldn't imagine growing up this way. Like Adam, I didn't consider *the sight* a gift. Maybe if I caught the thing killing my clients, then I'd reassess. Until then, it stayed firmly entrenched in the curse category.

Couldn't wait to see the look on Finn's face when I told him that the spell had worked. Mr. Nonbeliever himself was going to get a lesson in the supernatural that he wouldn't soon forget. Or maybe not. It was obvious that Finn had been hiding quite a bit from me. For now, confronting him would have to wait. I had to come up with a way to attract the thing I'd spent the last seven years trying to forget.

Adam wasn't sure it could be trapped. He'd never heard of anything like this Shade—spirit-bogeyman. He said the ghosts he'd spoken to were afraid of it. Apparently, *it* worked much like I used to. It would creep into a house and cleanse it. I never asked Adam how. I didn't want to know, for fear the truth would hit too close to home. Suffice to say, whatever we were dealing with, it wasn't liked by the living or the dead.

We batted ideas around over the next few days. Adam hadn't liked any of the plans I'd come up with so far, but had yet to come up with anything better. I wasn't exactly psyched about using myself as bait, but I didn't think anything else would draw the monster out.

It had been Gabe's idea, but I hadn't seen him around since the ceremony. Maybe he'd finally given up and moved on. Yeah, I know, not likely.

The Shade had been after me from the beginning. I figured we could speed the process up by sending out a psychic invitation. I'd pretend to cleanse Adam's house and see if that caught the Shade's attention. I'd be waiting when it arrived. We had no idea how long it would take or if it would even work, but we had to try.

Like Adam, I doubted we were dealing with a typical

Shade, since this one seemed fond of traveling with demons that wore the skins of little kids. I frowned at that. It hadn't done that when it killed my parents. There'd been no children accompanying it.

Had it planned to use me? Was I too old for it? Did the kids have to be a certain age? So far they'd all been under ten. Did that matter? I really didn't know.

I shuddered and opened the book Adam had borrowed from Finn. He'd been more than happy to send it via courier when Adam told him it was to catch Stephen's killer. Finn had made it clear when they spoke that he wasn't ready to see me yet. He was still too freaked out by what had happened and he wasn't ready to tell me the truth. The news had hurt my feelings, but I knew we'd eventually kiss and make up. Well, we'd at least make up—if I survived.

I scanned the pages quickly. I didn't know much about dark witchcraft, but there were a few spells in here that might work in summoning the creature and trapping it. I was just about to send Adam out for supplies, when I remembered the Talking board I'd owned as a kid. It had worked the first time. Would it do so again? It was worth a shot.

Adam walked into the room.

I put the book aside. "I need you to pick up a Talking board from the toy store when you go out. Oh, and some chalk so that I can draw the binding circle on the ceiling."

Adam tipped the book until he could see the page. "That symbol is used for trapping demons. You aren't after a demon."

"No, but one might show up, since they tend to when the Shade comes around. I'd like to be prepared just in case."

He looked exasperated. "I told you. It wasn't a Shade that killed Stephen and your clients."

I sighed. "Well, whatever it is, it seems to attract some nasty company."

Adam let go of the book. "I've never seen a demon in all

the years I've been doing this job. You'd think if they were around that I would've crossed paths with one by now."

"Funny, I thought the same thing and look where it got me." I caught his gaze. "Besides, you said that you couldn't see Huli Jing when she was standing six feet away from you."

Adam shook his head. "I couldn't."

"So maybe demons have been around and you just haven't been able to see them." It was good reasoning on my part. At least I thought so.

He looked thoughtful for a moment. "It's possible, but that still doesn't explain the creature you're after. You said the demons, with the exception of Huli Jing, looked like your clients' kids. But the other entity resembled a shadow man."

"He was thicker, but yes," I said. "You're the one who told me it wasn't."

"And I stick by my initial observation. It moves in the shadows, hiding. Uses them to hunt. I haven't been able to get a good look at it."

The color drained from my face. "You've seen it."

His eyes shuttered, hiding the blue depths. "I've seen..." His voice trailed off. "There's something in the shadows."

I rested my hands on the book and leaned forward to get a good look at him. "What shadows? What exactly are you talking about?"

Adam shrugged. "It's hard to explain. You have to see it for yourself to truly understand. There are shadows that exist in the realm of the dead. The departed won't go near them and I can't *see* inside of them. It's as if something is purposely masking its presence. I take the dead's advice and try to avoid them."

"Great, something else to look forward to in the future."

Adam smiled. "Fortunately, shadows are rare." He looked back at the book.

I picked it up and tilted it until he could see what I was

attempting to draw. "This was the only circle I could find in the book that was made to trap things. I have no choice but to use it. I want something powerful, strong enough to hold evil. I figure a demon is about as powerful as you can get. Anything else should be small potatoes by comparison."

He traced the image with his fingertip. "You're using an elephant gun on an anthill," he said.

With newfound determination, I said, "I'll use whatever I can get my hands on in order to take this thing down. I'm going for total annihilation. Don't you think it's done enough damage?"

Adam sobered at the reminder. "More than enough," he said. "I'll get everything you need. I'm sure the New Age bookstore will have some of the materials. They are well stocked. The hardware store will have the sheet steel. The rest I'll find at the toy store and in Chinatown."

"Yes, kids are the best clients for Talking boards," I mocked.

He cupped my cheek and warmth blossomed. "Be back soon."

"I'll be here."

Adam paused. "Are you sure that you feel up to this? We could always wait awhile longer."

The ritual hadn't hurt me, only freaked me out. "I'm feeling good. As ready as I'm ever going to be." I rolled my arm for emphasis.

Adam looked at the handprint on my shoulder, then at my face.

"It doesn't hurt anymore."

Concern clouded the blue of his eyes. "You heal unusually fast."

I know, but I couldn't think about that right now. I could only handle one problem at a time. "You'd better get going."

He brushed my lips in a feather soft kiss, then left.

I laid the magic circle face up on the table, then grabbed a piece of paper and began to draw. I wanted to practice a few times before I sketched it with the chalk.

There could be no mistake when I summoned seven-six-seven to Adam's house. Maybe I'd find out its real name before I killed it. I'd had second thoughts about using Adam's place, but he had insisted. I'd argued, but in the end he'd won. He'd been doing that a lot lately. Pretty soon he'd get tired of being right all the time. I grinned.

Maybe not.

Sketching the circle on the ceiling seemed the obvious choice. Most people don't look up. And if it did, I could always try to draw its attention down. Made perfect sense to my inexperienced mind.

Could Shades read? I suppose Ethyl and Bernie proved that they could, since they seemed to enjoy reading the paper with Adam, even when he didn't turn the pages fast enough to suit them.

I still wasn't used to them popping up around corners like a pair of sepia Weebles. It was creepy. They did seem to try to give me my space, for which I was extremely grateful, and I certainly went out of my way to avoid them. That didn't work as well, but we were trying for Adam's sake.

* * * * *

Adam returned two hours later with the supplies. I now had paper charms from Chinatown, which I needed to burn if Huli Jing made an appearance, chalk, batteries, walkie-talkies, and a divination board. The walkie-talkies hadn't been my idea, but Adam had insisted. He placed the sheet steel in front of his electronics. It wasn't as effective against an EMP shockwave, but it was better than nothing.

I set up the Talking board on his coffee table, then went to work on sketching the circle. I did it in black light chalk so that it would be less noticeable. It made the act of drawing more difficult and I had to stop on several occasions to shine a black light on the design to make sure that the symbols matched the page. While I worked, Adam wired his stereo to play the pop divas. All I had to do was press a button on the remote.

When I was finished, I stared at my handiwork and smiled. It wasn't half bad for a kid who never made it past seventh-grade art class. Hopefully that would do. If not… Well, I didn't want to think about what would happen, if my little Shade trap didn't spring shut.

It was disappointing to find out that even though I could see spirits now, I still couldn't touch them. So there would be no jumping the Shade or anything physical like that. I was stuck with using my regular equipment.

I glanced up at my handiwork. The book swore it was the strongest circle I could use. I blatantly ignored the section that said only a practicing magician should attempt this sort of spell. I might not be a magician, but I was a ghost hunter. That should count for something.

At least I thought it should. Not sure magic practitioners would agree. Good thing there weren't any of them around.

I'd made Adam promise me that he'd stay at my house tonight with Shaggy and the Finkelsteins. I couldn't take the chance that they'd be injured. He'd argued against it, saying that one phone call could bring in the whole Creep Squad to help.

I reminded him that we didn't know what we were dealing with and that until we did, the squad would be useless. Or worse—dead. I wasn't even sure the creature would show up if I weren't alone. In the end, Adam knew my plan was the only way to get this thing. I'd promised I would scream into the walkie-talkie if things got bad.

That was our signal.

If he heard me yell, he was to come running with my boom box and backup EMP device set to ten. I hoped it didn't come to that. I really did. I wasn't sure the pop princesses were strong enough to budge this thing.

And then there was Adam. He might talk to the dead and avenge them, but he'd never vanquished them. As a cop, he'd seen a lot of carnage, but I wasn't sure he'd have it in him to watch and listen to them writhe in pain before they dispersed. Other people on the squad were called in to take care of that aspect. Adam saved things. He didn't destroy them. That's just the type of person he was, and I liked him for it. I didn't want to be the one to change him.

I'd taken down the extra wards, so that Bernie and Ethyl could enter my home unharmed. I still didn't understand how they'd been able to get inside before without setting something off. But their answers had been cagey.

For added protection, Adam took what was left of the bag of salt from his backyard and sprinkled it around the foundation of my house after everyone was inside. He waved from the front porch and raised the walkie-talkie to his mouth.

"All systems go," he said. "Be careful."

I pressed the button and waved back. "You too. Take care of Shaggy for me."

I walked inside, shutting Adam's front door behind me. My gaze fell on the Talking board. And I couldn't stop the chill from tracking along my spine. It had been seven years since I'd touched one. Seven years since I'd *played* the game and invited seven-six-seven into my life.

Would I be able to do it again? I'd sworn after my parents' death that I'd never touch one of those evil boards again. I had made good on that promise, too. I broke the original one into seven uneven pieces and salted it to remove its power. I'd heard legends about Talking boards reassembling themselves and returning to their owners.

I knew they were probably just urban legends that came from horror movies, but I wasn't about to take the chance. Not after what I'd witnessed. It might not have been able to put itself back together, but it definitely held power.

I'd snuck into a church cemetery and buried the thing in a shallow grave on hallowed ground. Before my illegal nocturnal journey, I'd asked the minister to bless some flowers. Roses, from my mother's garden, which I promptly placed over the top of the board, trapping it. I buried one bloom deep, making sure it touched the pieces. Thankfully, the Talking board had stayed put.

Unlike the past, which refused to stay buried.

Chapter Fourteen

The lights were off in the house, when I summoned seven-six-seven. I'd lit several white and black candles. Adam's home now resembled a Goth club without the thumping tunes. My electromagnetic pulse device sat within easy reach on the table beside me, along with the remote control for the stereo and the walkie-talkie.

My hands shook when I placed my fingertips on the plastic planchette for the first time. The second I felt the planchette slide, the past collided with the present. And I gasped. So much pain. So much torment. And I was about to bring the whole thing to an end or die trying.

I ignored the gooseflesh rising on my arm and took a deep breath. This time I wouldn't be fooled by my own imagination. If something showed up, I'd see it. I rolled my head, then tried to relax while I waited for it to move again.

For an hour, I sat in the dark, smelling candle wax, asking if anyone was there, knowing good and well that no one was. My hands were stiff and the silence played tricks on my mind. Every creak or groan had my body tensing for an attack that never came.

It was only when a cool breeze brushed my neck that I

knew that I'd managed to summon something. I kept my hands on the planchette and attempted to casually glance around. No need to scare it away before I got a chance to trap and kill it.

My eyes scanned the darkness, watching the candlelight flicker from clear to blue, a sure sign that something was moving about the room.

"Is someone here? If so, could you please show me a sign? I would like for us to talk." I was about to ask again, when I spotted something emerging from the shadows. It was like watching the birthing process without the miracle aspect. My chest slammed into my ribs and my eyes began to water as fear gripped me.

The child toddled forward, his gait slightly off. The downward quiver wasn't a big giveaway. Most people wouldn't even notice the added motion. The *wrongness*. But I did.

It shone as clearly as the darkness surrounding him, closing in behind his wake. It was the only warning I'd get. The only warning I needed.

A hiss rattled the air. Snake? Or death's exhale? It didn't matter.

I lit the paper charms, fanning the flames to make them burn faster.

"Those are not meant for me, Gosling," Manuel Gonzalez said.

I shrugged. "I was expecting someone else."

"She will be here in a moment." I didn't see it move, but I felt the blow all the way to my toes. My body rocketed into the wall, shattering the chair I'd been sitting on. I got up dazed, but otherwise unhurt.

"Is that the best you got?" I taunted and reached for the remote. It flew to the opposite side of the room before I could grab it.

He tsked. "Do not test me, Gosling. You are in enough trouble as it is. Your need to hunt has left you teetering on the edge," Manuel said.

I found myself lifted into the air and tossed like a ragdoll over the coffee table and onto the floor. The breath whooshed out of my lungs and I gasped to fill them.

I scrambled to my feet. "You're the one who came in here looking for a fight."

He didn't answer. Instead, he sent a kitchen chair winging past my head. I barely had time to duck. I laughed when it crashed onto floor behind me. "Telekinesis. Neat trick." I didn't laugh long, when the second one hit its target, knocking my legs out from under me.

I landed hard, slicing my arm and forehead on the edge of the coffee table. Blood gushed onto the floor. One of my fingers was pointing at a ninety-degree angle. I grabbed it and yanked. Pain rolled through my body, leaving a wake of nausea behind. I cried out.

He hobbled forward. "Your behavior has forced us to take action. You cannot be allowed to continue harvesting unchecked."

I glanced at my clothes. "Do I look like a fucking farmer to you?"

His gaze focused on something behind me. I'd purposely kept my back to the wall, so there shouldn't be anything there. A giggle sounded in my right ear and gooseflesh prickled my arms and neck.

I rolled, but not fast enough. Huli Jing reached for my collar and pulled me up. It took a second for me to realize that she was levitating.

"You cannot get away," she said. "I made sure of that." Her dark gaze flicked to the burn beneath my shirt and pain scorched my flesh.

I struggled, pounding my fists down in an attempt to break her hold. She just smiled indulgently and rose higher until my head scraped the ceiling. My feet kicked, touching nothing but air as she backed me into the wall above the tropical fish tank.

Her tiny arm supported my body's sagging weight with ease. "What are we to do with you, Gosling?" she asked.

"Nothing," I gritted out between clenched teeth. "If you know what's good for you, you'll let me go."

She smiled. "If that is your wish," she said, then released me.

I plummeted, catching her arm at the last second, taking her with me. I'm not sure who was more surprised, Huli or me. We hit the saltwater tank together with a loud splash. The moment Huli's feet touched the warm water, her skin hissed like a lobster dropped into a boiling pot. The temperature of the water rose suddenly. She screamed and tried to scale my body to get out.

I pulled her against me until we were eye to eye. Fear flickered behind her empty eyelids. "Time to die," I said, then took a deep breath and submerged us.

Water flowed over the top of the tank and onto the floor as Huli struggled to break my grasp. Her cries continued underwater for a few seconds more, then slowly faded. Manuel bellowed and the glass tank shattered, spilling me onto the floor. I was still clutching what was left of Huli's lifeless corpse to my chest like she was a child's doll. I gulped air for a moment, then shoved her away, her flesh still sizzling from the saltwater bath.

The sound of the gasping fish tank pump filled the air. Between Huli's sizzles and the pump's gasps, it created a macabre kind of rhythm. Gasp, sizzle, gasp, sizzle, gasp.

When the sizzling faded, the demon scowled. "You will pay dearly for her death, Gosling."

"What do you want from me?" I asked, noticing a piece of metal sticking out the end of a broken chair leg. Desperate for any kind of weapon, I snatched it up. It was pretty poor in terms of protection, but it was all I had until I got to my EMP device. With it, I could drive him under the magic circle. He wouldn't be so tough once he was trapped.

I hoisted my broken body onto an elbow with a grunt and

tightened my grip on the iron shank. Pain shot through my arm, causing it to spasm and bleed. I held tight, ignoring the wetness pooling on the thick carpet beneath me. Fear whitened my knuckles. Frigid sweat beaded my forehead. My heart threatened to burst in my chest.

I wasn't going down without a fight.

I stared at five-year-old Manuel Gonzalez, attempting to see past the image of the baby I once knew. Something big and dark fluttered in the corner of the room, the flap of a thousand crows' wings taking flight. I sensed rather than saw it.

We were back to two against one.

Not fair, but that was nothing new. These things had fought dirty from the beginning. It was time that I did the same.

I'd get one chance to strike. Wounding Manuel didn't guarantee escape, but it certainly upped my odds.

Escape. I snorted. Who was I kidding? This kid was about to chew me up and floss with my entrails and there wasn't a thing I could do about it.

I scooted closer to the coffee table and groped for my EMP. I found it on my third try.

"Don't do that," Manuel warned.

I pressed the button and the skin on his little arms split like I'd sliced him with a filet knife.

He advanced on me. "I'm warning you."

I hit the EMP again, slashing his cheek. I clung to the fact that I had another way to fight them. The thought had barely crossed my mind, when an invisible hand yanked the EMP from my grasp and backhanded me across the face, splitting my lip and slicing my brow. I shook my head to clear it.

Storm clouds darkened his expression, until the fury was barely contained in his small body. He stepped forward, his tiny hands clenched into fists.

My grip tightened on the iron shank sticking out of the chair leg and I focused on his torso. At least I thought it was a torso. In this case, size was deceptive. I had no way of knowing if I was aiming at anything vital.

Manuel's skin dripped like candle wax, sagging on his bones in a loose fit. Like a child playing dress-up in his father's clothes, folds of pleated flesh gathered at his ankles, nearly tripping him.

Come on, you're almost there.

"It's not Manuel. It's not Manuel. It's not Manuel," I chanted under my breath as my mind screamed in protest.

Dark hair covered his brown eyes, but I had no doubt Manuel could see me. He could be blind and still find me with all the wheezing I was doing. I gasped, and tried not to cough.

The footsteps halted. Tiny feet encased in blue shoes with red racecars on top glared at me, illuminating the absurdity of the situation. He was still too far away.

"Just a little further, you son-of-a-bitch!" I glanced up at the circle on the ceiling. I wasn't sure if I'd suddenly grown a brass pair or if I had a death wish. Either way, I needed him to come closer.

Manuel canted his head much like a dog does, when you talk to them. He looked up and noticed the circle, then quickly bypassed it.

Crap! Now what was I going to do?

One thing was clear. Only one of us would get out of this alive. And I was determined that it would be me.

He took a step.

Yes.

This was it.

Keep it coming.

With more speed than I thought I was capable of, I shoved the iron shank deep, twisting as I buried the metal to the hilt into Manuel's tiny abdomen.

It wasn't Manuel.

It wasn't a child. I couldn't forget that. The road to sympathy was paved with the bones of the naïve. He was counting on my hesitation, my compassion, but I was fresh out.

A scream filled the air. I yearned to clasp my hands over my ears, but I didn't dare release the weapon. I bore down, using my weight as leverage. Windows shattered, walls shook, splattering green paint and white plaster onto the floor. The front door cracked down the middle, drunkenly hanging by its hinges.

Like a thousand talons attempting to gain purchase on a glass perch, the screeching sound grew in volume. Deafening. Pressure built in my body along my back. Either he was trying to get in or something was trying to get out. My skin burned. Flaming razors, slicing my shoulder blades.

I threw my head back and roared. "No!"

Fear welled, black, ugly, and snarling. I forced whatever it was back inside me by sheer will. The pain was excruciating. My vision dimmed. I shook my head to clear it. I couldn't pass out now or I'd be dead. Suddenly, the bones in my hand snapped. I toppled over like a flicked domino, clutching my wrist. A wounded cry, dying on my split lips.

Cheating bastard.

The iron shank made a sucking noise as invisible hands slowly pulled it out. It dropped with a dull thud onto the carpet, splattering black blood everywhere. The wound to his abdomen flamed outward, then began to burn.

Noxious sulfuric gas filled the air, choking my already oxygen deprived lungs. The fumes asphyxiated my thoughts, leaving me disoriented. Manuel reached for me, his small hands menacing despite their size. A red haze clouded my vision.

I knew I was about to die, but that didn't mean I had to stay here and wait for it.

If death wanted me—it would have to come and get me.

CHAPTER FIFTEEN

I dropped down and slithered on my belly, since I couldn't support my weight. Luckily, my blood and the saltwater made the motion easy.

"Where are you going, Alexa?" a deep voice asked. "The show was just getting interesting." He clapped as if I'd just taken a bow.

I froze in place. I was too hurt to fight another tiny titan. Wasn't killing one enough?

The demon in Manuel's skin hissed and backed away.

"You're not even going to acknowledge me? I'm disappointed, considering how much time and energy you've put into searching for me all these years."

My head snapped around. "Seven-six-seven?"

"At your service." He bowed in a surreal show of courtly manners that seemed incredibly out of place, considering the circumstances. His dark hair fell forward, glossy and thick, shading his pale face. He was taller than I'd remembered and quite a bit larger.

I'd painted him as a monster, when he looked like anything but. Of course, the last time I'd seen him, he'd been nothing more than a puff of black smoke with blue eyes, moving silent and deadly through my house. I wasn't fooled by his gentle appearance. He used his beauty to prey upon people.

"Please call me Ere," he said. "Seven-six-seven is so childish. Don't you think?"

Childish, yeah. It had been childish to think that I could play with something so dangerous and remain untouched. I'd been so naïve that I had actually thought this man, this creature, was my friend.

I wanted to tell him, but I didn't. He wouldn't care. He was incapable of such an emotion. Nothing I'd have to say would matter to this monster in civilized clothing. So instead, I asked, "Why the name change?"

He frowned. "Did you really expect my name to be a number?" he asked.

As a teen, I'd thought him calling himself a number was exciting. Kind of like *James Bond 007*. I'd forgotten about the license to kill part of the fantasy. "Why didn't you just tell me your name was Ere from the start?" I asked. "I wouldn't have minded."

"We were playing a game. The number enhanced the mystery. Besides, I was in a delicate position and names hold the power to control."

I made a mental note to look into the name thing if I survived. I shook my head and the room spun. I couldn't see the circle on the ceiling any longer. I knew it was there, but my eye was starting to swell shut. Would it work on Ere?

"I thought only demons appeared as numbers on a Talking board or is that an urban legend?" I'd read that in a book several years after my parents' death. Wish I would've known that before I bought the thing.

He shrugged. "Demons, or those who can summon them. I am the latter. Either Being can use simple numbers. The rules to which you are referring were written by men, not creatures of my world. They are guidelines and nothing more."

"Your world?" I looked around for emphasis. "Still looks the same to me."

"'Tis your world, too. All you have to do is reach for it and it'll be there for you," he said offhandedly.

My jaw clenched. "This is *my* world. The only world that matters. If you're not from here, then you're trespassing."

He looked as if he found our conversation tedious. "You should not take the word of man so seriously, Alexa. They are not reliable when it comes to recording history and are easily deceived."

I snorted. "You'd know all about deception. Wouldn't you? Speaking of which, I suppose you're here to finish off the job that your partner started," I said, only then remembering that Manuel was still in the room.

"My partner?" Ere asked, confused. "You mean the demon?"

I nodded.

Ere laughed long and hard. "I have no partner. Least of all a demon. You have it all wrong." He pointed to Manuel. "He's not here to help me. He's here to stop *us*."

"Us? There is no us," I ground out as a wave of pain hit, cramping my muscles. My body was hurting in places I didn't even know existed. "I can't believe that I've been getting my butt kicked by kids because they thought I worked with you."

Manuel took that moment to growl at Ere. "You shouldn't be here, winged one. This does not concern you."

Ere turned on him and I noticed for the first time black gossamer wings folded neatly against his back. The vision in Finn's den tumbled through my mind. It couldn't be. He couldn't be. If the children were demons, then what was he? He looked solid enough to touch, despite his shadowy form.

"Do not lecture me, little one." Ere took a menacing step forward.

The tiny fists clenched in anger. "Why don't you cross into the realm and we'll see who's the little one," Manuel challenged.

Ere hesitated. "I don't have time for this. Be gone."

"Just as I thought," Manuel said in a guttural voice. "Your bravery ends in this realm."

"Do not bait me, warmth carrier," Ere snapped. His wings fluttered in agitation.

Manuel held his ground. "You cannot have her. She has not crossed yet."

Crossed? I started replaying his words. Manuel was actually sticking up for me—sort of. But how could he, after I'd killed his partner and then stabbed him? No one was *that* forgiving. He rose to his full almost three-foot height, then squared his body and faced Ere. I was missing something. Something very important.

"Wait a minute," I interrupted, placing the fingertips of my left hand against the palm of my right. "Time out. I'm confused. If he's a demon, what are you?"

"He's a rogue seraph—an angel," Manuel said, without looking at me. "He plans to drag you into his bleak world where you will be pursued by hunters."

My brow furrowed. "Um, aren't angels supposed to be good?" I asked. Surely everything I'd ever been told or read about them wasn't wrong.

"So they'd like the world to believe," Manuel spat. "Nothing but a PR ploy. Had we hired a better public relations firm, we would be the ones adored by millions."

Angels? Demons? PR departments? They had to be yanking my chain. No way were angels and demons set up like corporations. "What about God?" I asked.

Manuel glanced at me. "He stays out of such matters. That's what the council is for."

If he was to be believed, then that meant the world was run by committee. No wonder it was so fucked up.

Ere motioned with his hand. "Leave, and take what's left of Huli Jing with you," he said. "Before I finish the job that she started. Alexa might not be strong enough to get you to the circle, but I am."

How could he have seen the circle? He hadn't been there long enough. Had he?

"The council will hear about this," Manuel vowed.

"I have no doubt." Ere chuckled. "Do you think I answer to the council?" he asked, stalking Manuel, driving him toward the circle. "I stopped playing by their rules over ten human years ago."

Manuel hissed, the sound trailing off into a snake's rattle. "You cannot convert a gosling who has no knowledge of our existence," he said.

Ere gave him an unholy smile. "I will not need to convert her. The hunger burning inside of her will bring her to me willingly. No one can resist it for long."

To prove his point, he flicked his wrist and power filled me, bowing my body toward him. I groaned, trembling in ecstasy as power shot through my weakened limbs. "Please," I pleaded, not sure whether I was begging him to continue or to stop.

"See, her body is weak," Ere said. "It's only a matter of time. Eventually she will succumb like I did. I'm sure you've heard the rumors."

Manuel's eyes widened and he took another step back. "So the whispers are true. I didn't want to believe it," he said.

Ere shook his head and raven hair fell about his broad shoulders. "Every last word."

Fear leached the last of the caramel color from Manuel's apple cheeks and he trembled. "You've left the seraph and crossed over to become a soul-eater."

Ere glanced at his hands. "You say that with such distaste, Munuane, but it's nice to see that you finally understand."

Munuane? Was that its real name? I was getting sleepy from the blood loss and finding it hard to keep up with their conversation. Pretty soon I'd need a playbook of who's who in the immortal realm.

Manuel—Munuane stood his ground. "I will give you one last chance to flee back to that frigid place you call Hell," Ere said.

"You do not rule this place, soul-eater. It is for all our kind. Or have you forgotten?"

Ere's expression could've frozen the Pacific as he glared at the demon. "I forget nothing, including this moment." Swirls of blue replaced his dark eyes. The smell of burnt paper filled the air. "I shall count to three. One. Two. Thre—"

The flames in the demon's eyes flared to life. "I'm going, but this is far from over," Munuane said.

Ere laughed. "Over? Hardly. This is just the beginning. Make sure you tell them that Los Angeles is mine, Munuane. I'd hate to think I spared your life for nothing."

The demon ignored him and looked at me. "Remember what I told you, Gosling. He will drag you down with him, if you let him." The child's image flickered like concentric rings on a lake, then slowly disappeared.

With Munuane gone, I had Ere's full attention. "Forgive the rude interruption. Now where were we?"

If he thought we were going to reminisce about old times, he was mistaken. "Why did you kill my clients?"

He shrugged, the movement graceful and at ease like we were chatting over tea. "It was the only way to drive you to me."

"Why now? It's been seven years. What took you so long?"

Ere seemed to consider his answer before speaking. "I had to give you time to develop a taste for the power that souls bring."

My stomach lurched. I opened my mouth to reply, but the words locked in my throat when Ere picked up the walkie-talkie. He pressed the button to speak and my voice came out of his mouth.

"Adam, please help me. He's going to kill me," he said, before crushing the device.

A dog barked. I recognized the tone instantly.

I gasped in shock. "What have you done?"

The bark was followed by a shout from Adam. "Shaggy, come back here."

Chapter Sixteen

Shaggy came bounding into the room a second later, past the broken door, teeth bared and hair high on his back. He was growling and barking. I'd never seen him act like that.

"Shaggy, no." I tried to crawl to him, but he lunged at Ere before I could reach him.

Shaggy's teeth clamped on Ere's wrist and something that looked like tar bubbled up on his skin, then began to ooze like chilled molasses. Ere's free hand clasped Shaggy behind the neck and pulled. Shaggy didn't want to let go. His bite was so firm that his jaws took a chunk of flesh with them as Ere ripped him away. He held him by the scruff of his neck, his legs dangling uselessly in the air.

"I take it this creature is yours?" he snarled in disgust and stared at my dog's face. Shaggy continued to snap viciously.

"Please don't hurt him. He was only trying to protect me," I begged.

His blue eyes hardened. "He made his choice."

Tears filled my eyes as Ere began to squeeze. Shaggy's whimpers grew louder and he struggled to get away.

"No," I yelled, crawling forward. "Stop! You're hurting him."

I didn't see Adam, until he was flying through the air. At first I thought he was going to tackle Ere, but at the last second, he snatched Shaggy from Ere's grasp. Unfortunately, the move wasn't quick enough to dodge the backhanded blow Ere delivered to the side of Adam's head.

Adam hurtled toward the wall unconscious, his arms still cradling my dog. He hit the wall with his back, then slid to the floor with a sickening thud. Blood trickled down the side of his temple and out of his mouth.

"That's it, you son-of-a-bitch. I've had it." I staggered to my feet, forcing my wobbly legs to support me, then straightened as much as the pain would allow. "This is our fight. Leave them out it."

"Fight?" Ere blinked, confusion plainly visible on his aquiline face. "Is that what you think?"

In that moment, he reminded me of Gabe, with his dark brooding eyes and perfectly sculpted features. Then he moved and I dismissed the thought as a trick of the candlelight.

I glanced at Shaggy and Adam. "You've given me no reason to believe otherwise."

"I didn't come here to fight with you, Alexa," Ere said.

I searched frantically for a weapon and spotted the discarded metal shank. "Then why did you come here? To hurt my dog? To hurt Adam?" Shaggy was curled up on his lap, licking his face. Adam didn't look like he was breathing. My heart clenched. "It sure as heck wasn't a social call."

"On the contrary, that's exactly why I came. Don't you recall the invitation you gave me?"

My throat constricted. I remembered all too well what had brought Ere into my life. I glanced over and spotted the Talking board on the table. Could I somehow send Ere back to wherever he came from? Doubtful, since I had no idea where that might be, now that my notions of heaven, hell, demons and angels had been tossed out the proverbial window.

He followed my line of sight. "A crude instrument, that." He nodded to the board. "I can't believe it led me straight to your parents. To you. There was a time I thought that I'd never find them."

"What?" My parents were innocent. They had nothing to do with this mess.

"They'd been in hiding for years. I'd almost given up."

Anger roared to life inside of me. I felt the same burning on my back that I'd repelled before. "You are a liar! My parents were never in hiding."

His eyes flashed a brilliant ice blue, before fading to soothing brown. "I am many things, but a liar is not one of them."

I could think of a lot of reasons to hide from something like Ere, but I couldn't think of a single one that would explain my parents' actions. "Why would my parents need to hide?"

He crossed his arms over his chest. "Because they'd broken the law."

"Now I know you're full of it. They were law-abiding citizens. My parents had never even had a parking ticket."

He sighed. "Not human law, the Seraphim law. The one that states no angel shall ever lie with a human. Thou shalt not lie with the unclean." Ere's lip curled in revulsion.

Denial burned my tongue. "You're lying. My parents were human."

He laughed. "Is that what they told you? No wonder you are so ignorant of our ways."

My parents hadn't told me anything. And why should they? I was human. They wouldn't have lied to me about something so important. "They didn't have to tell me. It was a given."

I flashed to a time when I was eight years old. I'd fallen on a broken rabbit hutch in our backyard. Blood had been everywhere. Mom had rushed out of the house and pulled me close. Her hand moved to the wound. Within seconds the pain had stopped and I was good as new. She'd told me it was mommy magic and that the scrape hadn't been serious. I'd believed her. I'd never thought about that moment again until now. I hated that Ere had me doubting my parents.

He stepped around the destroyed furniture, avoiding the circle on the ceiling. "You should've been raised as a Halfling. It would make things much simpler."

"Simpler for who? You're sick. You mess with people's lives and don't care about the consequences."

I couldn't seem to catch my breath. Ere had to be lying. I *was* human. My parents were human. My body began to tremble as I fought to control my emotions. He was wrong. He had to be wrong.

"That's it," he coaxed. "Let your true nature come out."

I gasped and doubled over in pain. When I could open my eyes again, my gaze landed on the broken chair leg. "This is my true nature." I dove for the shank and came up with it in my hands.

Ere's gaze dropped to my weapon. "What do you plan to do with that?"

"Kill you."

His lips twisted into a smile. "Now that would be a trick, seeing as how we can't harm each other."

"That's your second lie." I lunged, aiming the shank at his heart. It stopped a centimeter from his chest, refusing to enter. I shoved harder. The resistance matched the force I expelled.

He watched me dispassionately. "I told you that I do not lie."

"No, damn it." I pushed with all my strength, putting my body weight behind it. "Why won't you die?" I sniffled, determined not to cry.

He slowly shook his head, his lips quirked in amusement. "I told you, we cannot harm one another."

Tears filled my eyes. "But you killed my parents."

"That was different. I was within the law. The council

had given me a weapon tuned to your mother's angelic frequency. It's the only way for one of us to kill another. Your father was of little consequence, since he was human and easily destroyed."

He was discussing my parents' murder as if it were the evening weather report. "You sick bastard. I'll figure out a way to kill you, if it's the last thing I do."

He glanced at the Talking board and frowned. "I have no doubt you will try."

"And succeed," I spat. "Even if I have to make friends with every creepy crawly out there."

He brushed my cheek with the back of his hand. I shivered on contact. "Things with you are a little more complicated. Thanks to that toy, you and I are connected, but you already knew that. You've seen what I've seen. Felt what I've felt. Experienced the thrill of the kill through my eyes."

I recoiled in horror. The dreams I'd been having weren't dreams at all. They were visions. I'd blamed Huli Jing for that unwanted ability. It was one of the reasons I'd killed her. But they were Ere's doing all along.

"Sever the connection right now," I demanded. I didn't need to see his death home movies running through my head.

"If only I could." His attention shifted toward the door and his muscles tensed. "Listen, I don't have time to cover basic angelic law with you. I came here to ask you to join me."

Had he missed the part about me wanting to kill him? Or was he just mental?

He went to stroke my face again, but I pulled back before he could touch me. "I want us to join forces. Los Angeles isn't big enough for two soul-eaters," he said.

"I am not a soul-eater. Manuel said so." It didn't matter that I had no idea what it meant to be a soul-eater, I just knew I wasn't one. Not yet anyway.

He smirked. "You might not be one now, but you will be

soon. You've developed quite a taste for souls over the years. You crave their power. Even now your hunger grows."

It was horrible to think about. There was no way the power I'd felt from dispatching Shades had come from me eat—absorbing their souls. My stomach rolled and I swallowed hard to keep from retching. How could he—I was nothing like him.

"You're wrong about me," I said. "You're wrong about everything."

"You know that I am not. I can see the truth in your eyes. We are alike. And because of this, I cannot have you poaching on my territory. Unfortunately, I cannot dispatch you." He brushed my shirt aside to expose the handprint on my skin. "The burn on your shoulder presents another set of problems."

I reached for it subconsciously and rubbed. It was one of the few things on my body that didn't hurt.

"The mark allows the demons to track you by scent and keep tabs on your ghostly activities. If you hunt, they'll know it. It's been weakened by the death of Huli Jing, but it will never disappear completely. So that leaves us only two choices. We can both make nice and join forces so that we're too powerful to defeat or we remain estranged and eventually figure out a way to destroy one another. What say you?"

"Go fuck yourself." I kept my expression neutral. I didn't like the idea of having permanent demon BO, but since I'd killed the only creature that could remove it, I'd have to learn how to deal. It was nice to know that Ere and the demons weren't indestructible.

Ere's jaw tightened. "Is that your final answer?" He looked at the door again as if he expected to see someone at any moment.

"Yes," I said.

"Pity, we'll have to see if I can't change your mind." He

had the audacity to wink. "I must go now. We're about to receive a visit from an uninvited guest. Gabriel always was a pain in my feathers." Ere's image morphed into smoky shadows. "We'll continue this some other time," he said, and then he was gone.

I glanced at Shaggy and Adam. The urge to stay was strong. I loved Shaggy and I cared for Adam. He'd saved my dog's life. I knew that they needed help desperately. But I'd waited seven years to have a chance to catch Ere and I couldn't let him slip through my fingers.

"I'm sorry. Please forgive me," I murmured, then took off out the door.

I ran around the house and saw Ere heading toward the fence. "Come back here, you coward." I pushed myself harder. I wasn't like him no matter what he said. I didn't go around destroying people's lives.

No, but you're leaving your injured friends to pursue your own needs.

I stumbled at the sound of my conscience spouting off, but caught myself before I fell. The black mist in front of me accelerated. We were nothing alike. Nothing.

Bending at the waist, I stopped to catch my breath. He was wrong. Ere had to be wrong. The Talking board did not connect us. I refused to be connected to the monster that had destroyed my family.

No matter what he said, I would not end up like him and I'd prove it, starting now. A shadow streaked past me, barely missing my head. I ducked, but still felt something touch my hair. It was just a brush, but suddenly I didn't feel as bad as I had a moment ago.

Gabe...

As if the thought summoned him, I heard his voice on the wind. "If you aren't going to hunt, Gosling, then I suggest you stay out of my way," he said, then added, "You're welcome."

Part of me wanted to flip him off again, but I was grateful

for the healing. I prayed that he caught Ere and nailed his wings to a board. I stood there watching the shadowy streaks until they faded from sight, then returned to the house.

The sky lightened as I reached what was left of Adam's front door. I stood, staring at the houses across the street as the sun peeked over the rooftops, feeling more lost than I ever had.

Shaggy whimpered. I pulled myself away from the door and brushed the tears that had started to fall with the back of my sleeve. I reached for the phone and dialed 911, then rushed over to help.

The ambulance arrived seven minutes later. Fueled by my raging guilt, the short time felt like an eternity. As soon as I heard the paramedics say that Adam was stabilized, I was able to breathe again. I raced Shaggy to the emergency veterinary hospital, only pausing at red lights. They both entered surgery twenty minutes later, leaving me alone to confront my personal demons and take a long, hard look at my life.

CHAPTER SEVENTEEN

Adam and Shaggy came through their surgeries without complications. I hadn't bothered to go home, choosing instead to rush back and forth between the vet and the hospital. I still couldn't believe that Adam had risked his life to save my dog. Something in the vicinity of my heart melted. I owed him big time and didn't know if I'd ever be able to repay him.

He awakened from surgery three hours later, groggy, but in good spirits. "Did you get him?" he asked.

I shook my head, unable to say the words.

"It's okay." Adam squeezed my hand. "You can get him next time."

Leave it to Adam to try to make me feel better, when he was the one lying in the hospital bed.

"Alexa?"

"Sorry," I said, meaning it. "I'm so sorry I got you into this mess."

Adam frowned. "What was he?"

My gaze dropped away. "I'm not sure he was telling the truth," I said, not answering the question.

Adam sat up with a wince. "What did he say?"

I pulled away from Adam's grip and walked to the window. "He said that he was an angel. Can you believe that?" I glanced back with a smile pasted on my face.

Adam grew quiet. "Do you believe him?"

I ran a hand through my hair. "I don't know what to believe anymore. I've seen so many things over the last few weeks that I don't know which end is up."

He groaned in pain.

I rushed to his bedside. "Should I call the nurse?"

"No." He gave his head a quick shake. The movement caused his face to turn green.

I pressed his shoulder onto the bed. "Stop moving," I said.

Reluctantly, he settled. "Do you know what he wants?"

I nodded. "Yes, he was quite specific."

Adam watched me closely. "Am I going to like the answer?"

"No." I shook my head. "You're not."

He tried to sit up straighter.

"Please stay still. You're going to rip your stitches open," I said as he groaned again.

His blue eyes were slightly glazed from the drugs when they met mine. "What about the demons?" he asked.

"It's a long story." I shrugged. "I managed to kill Huli Jing, using your fish tank as a weapon, but there are a lot more where she came from." My face heated. "I'll pay you back for the tank."

"Don't worry about the fish tank. I'm just glad that you're all right." His expression grew pensive, but he didn't speak. After a while the drugs kicked in and Adam's eyes drifted closed. I watched the steady rise and fall of his chest. The muscles in his face had relaxed and Adam looked years younger than his twenty-something age. Peace settled over his features. I didn't want to wake him, so I tiptoed out of the room.

I decided to head home and grab a quick shower. I was

tired and I stank of dried blood. I'd told the police that Adam would explain everything once he recovered.

There was so much to digest and to consider. My mind was so awhirl with thoughts that I didn't notice that my front door was unlocked until I stepped into my living room and spotted Gabe.

He was seated on my couch with his long legs propped up on my coffee table. He had an old tome about demons resting on his chest. He finished the sentence he'd been reading, then glanced over the top of the book to look at me.

"It's about time you returned," he said. "This is a fascinating read, albeit quite outdated. Demons don't really have horns and breathe fire, but they can produce quite a bit of internal heat. I'm sure you know that already, though, since your skin holds the slight odor of their stench. It was smart of them to plant a tracking wound on you. That way they can keep an eye on you, when I can't."

"Can you remove it?" I hoped that Ere had lied when he'd said it would never go away.

Gabe grinned. "No."

"Surely you have some kind of angelic deactivator or cleaner tucked in your coat somewhere."

He chuckled. "Even if I did, I wouldn't remove it."

I slipped my coat off and tossed it onto the leather chair. "Terrific. Since you're not here to help, then you must have stopped by for some other reason."

He arched a brow as if to say, 'It would be a cold day before that would happen.' "Can't I drop in simply to visit? Perhaps I just wanted to see if you were okay."

"Is that why you're here?"

"No," Gabe said.

Why was I even having this conversation? It was like I'd been tossed into a Japanese production of *Hamlet* and told to quote lines. "Why didn't you tell me who you were? What you were? Why did you have to lie? You led me to believe that you were a ghost hunter, too."

He stared at me, his expression puzzled. "What exactly do you think I am?"

I shrugged. "Heck if I know. It's been a long night. Since you were chasing Ere, I'll assume you're some kind of angel hunter."

He almost looked hurt by what I'd said, but I knew it was an act. They were all masters of illusion. Deception was second nature to them. "I do far more than hunt." He lifted his feet off the coffee table. "I wanted to tell you, but then I realized that you knew nothing of your heritage. In the end, it wasn't my place."

I snorted. "Two more innocents almost died and it wasn't your place to tell me the truth?"

Gabe put the book down and stood. "I couldn't tell you. There are rules that must be followed, especially with one so near to turning as yourself."

I glared at him. "I'll tell you what I told Ere. We are *nothing* alike."

His gaze softened. "The power that comes from the kills is alluring. Some would say addicting. I had to find out if you could control the urges or if they were going to control you."

The word *soul-eater* whispered through my mind and I shivered. The power *was* addicting. I craved it just like Ere had said I would. The thought that he might be right left me feeling ill. "Are you telling me that this was some sort of friggin' test?"

Gabe gave me a curt nod. "In a fashion."

I fought to curb my anger, but that didn't stop my good hand from curling into fist. "What would've happened if I'd failed?"

His expression closed down. "Then I would've had to kill you. Just like I will Ere, once I catch him."

Heat flooded my face. "You're both sadistic bastards!"

His eyes glittered, flitting from brown to blue and back again. I realized the change in color indicated his emotional state. "Don't say things that you do not mean," he warned.

"Oh, I mean it," I said, then swung at his jaw. He caught my fist in his hand easily and squeezed enough to let me know that he could crush the bones, if he'd wanted to, but he didn't release me. "I had no idea what was going on. Even with Ere's explanation, I still don't understand. How can I be half angel and not know it?"

Gabe stepped closer, crowding me. "Ignorance does not excuse your actions."

I tried to pull away, but he wouldn't release me. "Why am I not surprised? Kill it and ask questions later is your response to everything."

"I could say the same about you." He rubbed his thumb over my knuckles and heat flared between us. "It would be my duty to dispatch you, but I would not find pleasure in the act."

I jerked again to no avail. "Is that supposed to make me feel better? If so, that's messed up. I thought angels were supposed to be compassionate and kind. Tell me, are angels born liars or is it something that you all learned how to do over the years?"

He arched a magnificent brow and gave me a casual shrug, effectively dismissing my outburst.

"I want you out of my life and out of my house, before I do something that we'll both regret."

He laughed. The sound sent delicious tingles down my spine, despite my resolve to hate him. "I'm afraid the first request is not possible."

"It's a great big world out there. Pick somewhere else. I'm not asking, by the way. I'm telling you. Leave now or prepare to get your feathered butt kicked from one side of the room to the other."

Gabe stared at me. "Just because I healed you doesn't mean you're in any condition to act upon that threat," he said. "Besides, my job here is not finished."

"You've already let the bad guy get away, and you've

threatened my life. What more is there to do?" I held up a finger. "Oh wait, let me guess. You have to stick around a little longer to see if I'm going to flip out and become a soul-eater."

He stroked my knuckles again. Heat curled in my belly and I swayed toward him. "No. That, my dear Alexa, is something that I do not want to see. It would be somewhat disappointing." He stepped closer, his cool breath fanned out over my face as he exhaled. Our bodies were mere inches apart. "My task is still the same. I will continue my pursuit of our mutual acquaintance until I have apprehended or dispatched him."

My blood chilled. There was no way I was going to let Gabe get anywhere near my angel. "I told you when we met that the rogue was mine. He killed my parents."

"Yes, I know. I am sorry. That was a slight overreaction given their crimes. The rules have relaxed a bit since then. I would've at least brought them before the council had I been charged with their apprehension."

I gave him a pained laugh. "Oh, that makes you so much better than he is. Whatever helps you sleep at night."

Gabe ignored the jab. "I *am* better than Ere." He puffed out his chest. "I have chosen not to let the hunger sway me."

I tried to pull my hand away, but he held firm. "Whatever, dude." I shrugged.

"How do you plan to kill him?" he asked. "Are you going to use your connection to Ere to track and kill him?"

"He says I can't kill him, but I'm not convinced," I said. "Now that I know what's going on, I need you to stay out of my way."

His sensual lips parted alluringly. "Not possible," he said. "I intend to get to him first."

"Listen, you overgrown feather duster, I'm warning you to back off." I took a step forward and we touched. My eyes rounded as the sensual awareness that had been sparking between us burst into flames. I jumped back, but not before seeing the interest in his eyes.

Gabe's mouth canted as he fought back a smile. "No need for *hostilities*. Ere won't surface for a while. I injured one of his wings before he could make good on his escape."

His declaration stopped me short. Gabe had managed to injure him. That was more than I'd been able to do. I refused to allow myself a moment of admiration. Awesome hunting skills or not, Gabe hadn't earned my respect. If anything, I owed him contempt.

"I won't hesitate to take you out if you get between me and Ere. I mean it, Gabe. I will figure out a way to kill you guys just like I did with the demons. Do not underestimate me."

His fingers curled gently around my shoulders, warming them, before pulling me against him. "Never that, Gosling," he said.

Gabe's beautiful eyes flashed blue fire a second before his lips descended. It was him. He was the one I'd seen in my vision during the Solomonic rites. He'd caught me. Protected me from the flames. Now he was fanning them. I couldn't move. Couldn't seem to catch my breath. And when I did, I inhaled his deliciously cool scent.

So masculine. Overpowering. Seductive. The razor-sharp teeth flashed in my mind.

And deadly.

I could never allow myself to forget how dangerous he was or the fact that he wouldn't think twice about killing me.

My sense of self-preservation kicked in and I turned away. His lips brushed my cheek instead. It was like a shock to the system. One that I tried desperately to ignore. Gabe slowly released me. I looked at him, expecting to see the sting of disappointment. His taunting smile told a different story. If he wished it, I'd still be wrapped in his arms.

My hand shook as I touched my lips with my fingertips. They were still tingling in anticipation like I'd received a low level static shock just by being near him. I'd felt something similar when he'd touched me at the Gonzalez family home and healed my shoulder.

"You don't want me to finish healing you?" he asked, being purposely obtuse.

I shook my head. "I thought you already did. And you didn't need to kiss me to do it. Don't ever try that again."

His expression changed to one of challenge. "I can make no such promise," he said, all mocking gone from his tone.

When you get used to lies, the truth can be shocking. I knew I shouldn't ask, but I had to know. "Why did you even try?"

Gabe licked his lips as if he were savoring something decadent. "Because I wanted to taste you. I've heard that goslings taste unique." His eyes sparkled and his voice dropped. "I wanted to see for myself."

He had been toying with me again. I should've known this was one big game to him. Maybe that's how angels rolled.

"Get out," I hissed under my breath, because I couldn't seem to find my voice after that near miss.

He grinned. "As you wish, Gosling."

I stomped childishly. "Stop calling me that."

He strode toward the door, then paused, shooting a glance over his shoulder. "I'll have my eye on you. I won't hesitate to carry out the sentence of our people, if you start to turn into a true soul-eater."

I glared back. "Know this, hunter: If you get between me and the rogue, you're going down. I will find a way. There has to be a cookbook somewhere that details how to pluck an angel."

Gabe laughed. "I look forward to our next encounter." His gaze swept my body and for a moment I knew he wasn't talking about fighting.

"Don't let the door hit you in your feathered ass on the way out."

He grinned, and then disappeared.

I staggered to the couch. His warmth still permeated the leather. I shot up, feeling singed, and thought I heard Gabe chuckle. I brushed at my clothes to wipe away his scent. I could still feel his hands on my body. I was mortified that I'd actually wanted him to kiss me. This was the second time that had happened.

"Bastard," I muttered under my breath and strolled into the kitchen to put on a pot of coffee. After my shower, I'd head over to the vet's one more time to check on Shaggy, then go back to the hospital. I wasn't good at sitting around twiddling my thumbs, but my impatience wasn't going to speed up their recovery.

Adam and I had been naïve enough to believe that we could trap demons or angels. Of course, we hadn't known it was an angel—much less a rogue angel—when I'd come up with the plan. I thought I'd understood what we were up against. Nothing could've been further from the truth.

All the books that I'd ever read on the subject were wrong. I would need to throw them out and start over. How could my parents have kept such a secret without me knowing about it? This was something I needed to know, had a right to know. Their omission hurt and left me vulnerable in a world I couldn't begin to understand.

A world that would get me killed if I made the wrong move or broke a hidden rule. I was amazed I'd made it this long without someone like Gabe coming after me.

Eventually I'd need to find out more about angels and demons. Especially now that I knew I was one. Even thinking it sounded ridiculous. Me, a half-angel. The world was going to hell in a hand basket for sure. Either that or somebody had a heck of a sense of humor.

I thought about my upcoming search. It wasn't like I'd be able to go to the library and find a text on the subject. Which meant one thing: I'd eventually have to ask Gabe for help. And he knew it.

No wonder he'd been so smug when he left.

* * * * *

Shaggy and Adam came home two days later. Adam teetered on crutches around my house, since I'd insisted that he stay with me until the doctor said he was well enough to walk without them. There was also the little fact that his house now needed extensive repairs, thanks to the demon smack-down. In the end, he hadn't put up much of a fight. I wouldn't admit it, but it was nice having someone around.

Ethyl and Bernie popped by on occasion to look in on him. Like protective parents, they fawned over Adam. They'd stay until they caught a glimpse of me, then there would be a pop followed by a cinnamon fragrance and they'd disappear. I still made them nervous.

The feeling was mutual.

Shaggy was doing much better, considering he was stuck inside the cone of shame again. He'd try to scratch and bite himself, only to be knocked back by the cone. The cast on his paw didn't help matters. After every rebuff he'd turn and look at me with those soft brown puppy dog eyes. I'd taken about a half-dozen doggy guilt trips so far and I knew I had a month's worth at least ahead of me.

"I'm sorry, boy," I crooned, giving his back a quick brush with my nails.

He looked at me and then slunk away.

"He'll forgive you, once they remove that cone," Adam said.

I hoped he was right. I didn't want my dog hating me.

Adam's cell-phone rang. "Excuse me," he said, then answered.

I walked into the backyard to give Adam some privacy. My roses were still in full bloom, their yellow petals as cheery as ever. My heart skidded in my chest as I recalled my mother's garden being eerily similar.

So there had been signs after all, if you knew where to look. I just hadn't known. Hadn't even suspected the truth. I inhaled the once comforting fragrance and tried to relax. My mind drifted to Adam, Finn, and the Paranormal Friends Society.

I knew I should keep my friends close so I could watch over them, but I wasn't sure if that was prudent. Look what had happened the last time I'd done that. Stephen was murdered and Adam was injured. I knew that danger came with his job. You couldn't be a cop without courting danger, but the knowledge didn't make my decision any easier. The next time Adam might not be so lucky.

I couldn't bear it if anything happened to him or to Finn.

I heard the off kilter strides of Adam's approach.

"Is everything all right?" I asked, without turning.

He swung himself around on the crutches until he was facing me. "That was the chief of the Paranormal Investigative Task Force."

I stared at his shiny new crutches. It would be weeks before he was fit for duty again. "They're not sending you back out already. Are they?"

Adam gave me a sheepish look. "He wanted me to ask you if you'd be interested in a job."

"Me?" I laughed. "Why would the police want me?" I didn't like mornings or following orders.

"You may be a civilian, Alexa, but you have more ghost-hunting experience than all the rookies combined. We could really use your help."

I toed the grass at my feet. "I don't know, Adam. I have zero police experience, unless you count my arrests."

"They'd be willing to train you," he said. "And it isn't like you wouldn't know anyone. I'd be there." He smiled.

It was tempting. I'd never thought about turning my calling into a genuine profession. I'd eked out a living. Not a good one, but I'd managed to keep a roof over my head. Still, being part of the PITF squad wouldn't leave me much time to hunt Ere. I'd told Adam what had happened, but I hadn't told him everything.

How could I go to work for the Creep Squad, knowing

what I knew now? "I'm sorry, Adam. I don't think so."

I had to stay as far away from temptation as possible. Of course, that left one small problem. How was I going to make a living if I didn't hunt ghosts full-time? I sure wasn't going to use my drywall license. That didn't leave a lot of choices.

Adam was watching me. "What if I said you could do the job part-time?"

Could I help with investigations part-time and still remain myself? "Your chief would agree to that?" I asked.

He nodded. The bruise on his face was still black, but it was beginning to fade. "If that's the only way he could get you, then absolutely."

My nerves tangled inside of me. If I accepted his offer, I wouldn't have to skirt the law. There was a slight risk that I'd be exposed to more souls, but it was minimal compared to the gain.

The Creep Squad was privy to information that Finn and the Paranormal Friends Society could only dream about acquiring. Their database encompassed every myth, legend, and bit of lore that existed on the planet. It could hold the key to finding Ere and dispatching him. I realized that I'd have to risk my well-being, if I wanted to put an end to this nightmare.

"Okay," I said. "I'll give it a try. Work freelance for a while to see if the job agrees with me."

He leaned forward and kissed me. It was a gentle brush, in no way demanding. "Good. I'll let him know." He hobbled back toward the house and I followed.

Adam made his call and set up a time for me to train. I never thought that life would take me in this direction. But then again, I never thought that there'd turn out to be angels and demons and I'd be one of them.

Sometimes life was a real bitch.

When Adam hung up, he texted me the information I'd need to start my new job. "Now that you know there are other creatures in the world, are you going to leave the ghosts alone?" he asked.

I had to smile. Adam was nothing if not persistent. I also knew that he was thinking about Ethyl and Bernie. He shouldn't have worried. I wouldn't go after them or any other Shade now that I knew what the consequences were. I could fight the hunger no matter what Ere and Gabe said. "The *Shades* are safe—for now."

"Good." He grinned back. "Glad to hear it. I'm looking forward to having you on my team. Of course, you'll have to answer to me on the job. Do you have a problem operating beneath me?"

The sexual innuendo sizzled between us, growing thicker by the second. "I think I can manage."

I walked to the door and stopped as my fist clenched the cool brass knob. Glancing over my shoulder, I caught his gaze. Adam looked as rugged as ever and beyond pleased with himself. I hated to take that glow of triumph away.

"Where are you going?" he asked.

"Finn's house."

He frowned. "Why?"

"I may be finished with Shades, but it's open season on rogue angels."

Emotion infused his expression, pouring out of his blue eyes in waves. It hit me, nearly taking my feet out from under me. I fought to stay afloat. It was an emotion I wasn't prepared to see or face yet. He looked so helpless on those crutches. Shaggy limped up beside him and sat with a whimper, completing the downtrodden picture.

"I don't want anything to happen to you," Adam said, his voice low and pained.

His words hurt almost as much as the burn from the demon. "That makes two of us," I said, going for levity.

Adam's face dropped, shuttering his beautiful eyes. "Alexa, I mean it. You could be killed. These things aren't like the spirits that you're used to dealing with." He ran a trembling hand through his hair. Making him sexier, if that were even possible.

I clutched the door. "I know."

Thanks to Gabe's cool touch and the angelic blood running through my veins, I was completely healed. I knew I wasn't indestructible, but I was far more bulletproof than the people I cared about.

I held Adam's gaze, feeling the lick of heat I got every time he looked at me. Temptation rose before I could stop it. Would that ever go away? Somehow I doubted it. Adam was a good man. He deserved a good woman, but for now, he was stuck with me.

Part of me longed to tell him that I'd give up my old *hunting* ways and that we could stay here in our safe neighborhood and live happily ever after, but I knew that was a lie. And I was done lying to Adam, and to myself. He deserved better. So I did the only thing I could do. I told the truth.

"The jury is still out on demons, but you're right, both sides are dangerous. Particularly rogue angels. Even knowing what I know now about these creatures, I could be killed. There's no denying the facts."

He nodded. "I'm glad you've come to your senses—"

"But—" I said, cutting off his words abruptly. "Not if I kill them first."

What had started out as revenge against Shades over a senseless killing, had somehow turned into a calling. And I was more than willing to answer. Back then, I didn't know that angels or demons existed.

Now, I did.

Made me wonder what else was out there, lurking in the shadows of night, waiting for an opportunity to spring forward and take a big bite out of me.

I decided I should go find out. Far be it from me to keep them all waiting.

Thank you for taking the time to read The Ghost Hunter Chronicles (Pt. 2): Ashes to Ashes. If you enjoyed the book, **LEND IT** to a friend. All my books are lending enabled. If you really loved Alexa's story, then please consider leaving a **REVIEW**. For more information about T.R.'s upcoming books, sign up now for her *newsletter*.

(http://trallardice.us9.list-manage.com/subscribe?u=0319c86af06494d0c92ae35d6&id=9e37a3a4ae)

IF YOU HAPPENED TO MISS
GHOST HUNTER CHRONICLES (PT1):
PLAYING WITH FIRE,
HERE'S A BRIEF EXCERPT

It's a strange sensation when the *dead* occupy a space. The utter stillness and unnatural cold can play tricks on a person's mind, bringing out a primitive side that most of us try to hide.

Naïve people believe that ghosts are harmless entities who've gotten lost on their way to the light.

Not me.

I know the truth. I know what they really are—parasites. They live off memories and fear until their hosts are sucked dry of their will to live.

That's why I don't try to coax, whisper, or talk to the dearly departed. I'm not there to help them cross over. At least not in the way most people think. I leave that crap to the others.

I'm there for one reason, and one reason only, to make sure the dead—stay dead.

My name is Alexa Dawn and I am a ghost hunter.

163

* * * * *

Should've known the day was going to be bad, since it started with a damp chew toy stuck between my toes. I'd received a call from a frantic couple claiming to have an ectoplasmic freak-out happening in their home. Normally, I take the time to validate a haunt before I jump into a job, but my rent was due and my dog needed kibble so I made an exception.

Unlike some of the places I'm called to in Los Angeles, the Frank Lloyd Wright rip-off wasn't dilapidated or historic. In fact, the McMansion looked new.

That told me two things. The first was that the haunt wasn't structure-based. It was somehow associated with the land or an object. The second was that this job was going to be a real bitch.

Land based ghosts do not like to leave peacefully. They throw tantrums that would shame any two-year-old on a sugar binge. The thought of being able to kick some ill-tempered specter butt brought a smile to my face. I could almost feel the buzz and I hadn't even dispatched it yet.

Some people take drugs to get high, I kill Shades.

Parking my truck in my new clients' driveway, I climbed out and glanced at the couple huddling in the center of the lawn. They were parked under a red umbrella and had on winter parkas. Since this was Southern California, I wondered how cold it was in their house.

I ambled across the lawn and stopped short of the umbrella. "I'm Alexa Dawn. You called earlier."

They looked at me and frowned.

"You're just a kid," Mr. Chang said.

I'm twenty, but I know I look a *lot* younger. There wasn't anything I could do about it.

They stared at my pierced eyebrow, then their gazes dropped to my ripped jeans and biker boots. The longer they stared, the higher their eyebrows went.

"I'm going to grab my equipment, then go inside and take

a quick look around. Be back in a few," I said.

"It's not safe," Mr. Chang said.

"It rarely ever is," I said, trying to shake off the unease their warning had instilled in me…

As I walked to my truck, Mrs. Chang muttered something that sounded like Fei Yen to Mr. Chang. He pulled her closer and told her everything would be okay. Since they weren't talking to me, I decided to get on with the job.

There are reasons why I don't normally accept work without researching the site. The very first job I was called out on involved an angry poltergeist. It was in Orange County, California, not far from where I grew up.

The two-story house was in an affluent neighborhood that barely managed to escape being devoured by the urban sprawl surrounding it. A tiny island of originality in a sea of sameness.

At the time, I had no idea what I was doing. The Shade sent me headfirst out a second-story window onto the front porch roof. I missed overshooting it by inches and broke my right arm in three places. I was lucky that was all I broke. And even luckier that the house had a front porch. Not many did in Orange County.

This was before I'd found the Paranormal Friends Society and learned a few advanced ghost-hunting techniques. I don't claim to be an expert, but despite my age, I am good at my job.

I gave Mr. and Mrs. Chang a reassuring nod, then stepped over the threshold into their home.

Priceless paintings hung in gilded frames above tables adorned with Asian antiquities. All the pieces looked well-chosen. The cultures and time periods blended seamlessly. That didn't mean that something nasty hadn't attached itself to one of the items, but it did make it less likely. It's a known fact in ghost-hunting circles that some antiquities don't play well with others. Think of it as a personality conflict.

My eyes told me that I was alone, standing in an opulent foyer straight out of *Architectural Digest*. But my senses …my senses knew better. Alive with anticipation, they waited patiently for that one proverbial twig to snap, the breeze to shift, the telling sign that would indicate the direction of the oncoming attack.

Make no mistake, it was coming. Death circled above me on invisible wings. Each flap bringing me closer to the inevitable. Except I planned to get out of this encounter alive.

I set my steel-encased boom box down on the marble checkerboard floor and ran my hands over my arms to dispel the gooseflesh, then yanked the ends of my leather jacket together. I zipped it as a shiver rattled my teeth.

One thing about cold spots: Once experienced, they were never forgotten. Much like smelling your first dead body or losing your virginity.

Yeah, it's that pleasant.

I took a deep breath and let it out slowly, attempting to get a sense of the house. I'm not psychic, but it was amazing what you could pick up if you just paid attention. Energy had a pulse. Slower than a heartbeat, but just as steady.

It throbbed through my body, giving me insight into the environment. It let me know when it was safe and warned me when it wasn't. Energy was always there, floating beneath the surface. Most people just didn't pay attention until it was too late.

This home's beat was thready and uneven as if the life was being slowly drained from its cream-colored walls.

I sniffed, inhaling the sickly sweet odor wafting in the air. Ginseng? Burnt sugar? Sandalwood maybe? Bloodhound, I'm not.

Over the years I have learned to identify quite a few fragrances in an instant. Flicker ghosts, the kind you catch out of the corner of your eye, smell like raisins, while poltergeists are sour like sunbaked milk.

Each odor had a story to tell. Sometimes the smell was the only way to determine what kind of spirit you were dealing with. You didn't want to think that you were banishing the spirit of gentle Aunt Tess and end up with Jack the Ripper. The former would leave in a whisper, while the latter would try to live up to its namesake. I preferred to deal with the Jacks of the world. They were loaded with siphoned energy.

I inhaled deeply again and exhaled slowly. It was important to determine the scent. Every time I thought I had it, the odor changed, becoming elusive. Strange. Shades didn't do that—couldn't do that to my knowledge. I didn't like that I couldn't pin down the scent. I should've been able to identify it, at least on the second try. Unease settled on my shoulders, knotting the muscles.

Relax. You're just tense because it's been awhile.

Everything in the environment holds some clue as to what's happening in a home. This house was no exception. Eventually, it would reveal its secrets. I just had to be patient.

Three red doors spaced ten feet apart lined the left wall like Canadian Mounties at attention. Three more lay directly across the room, mirroring their placement. Why red doors? Why not blue or white?

I knew in some Asian cultures red was considered a lucky color, while white was funerary. Why hadn't the good fortune worked for my new clients, the Changs? Had they decorated based on personal taste or beliefs? I should've asked. It makes a difference.

Taste was weak—but belief, belief held power.

I pulled two incense sticks, frankincense and myrrh, out of my tackle box and lit them, waving the sticks in the air to distribute the smoke. The combo might not be able to banish spirits completely, but the spicy fragrances had been known to calm Shades long enough for me to evict them.

When enough incense filled the air, I reached into my

pocket for the herbs I carried to every job. I scattered dill, fennel, mullein, and salt like birdseed across the floor. The mixture would prevent the Shade from moving from room to room. I was in no mood to play "chase the ghost."

Something about the home design made me uneasy. My brow furrowed as I studied the lines, color, and layout some more. The pattern reminded me of something I'd seen before. I mentally marked out the distance between the doors. It was *perfect*. Too perfect. An alignment like this could create a grid.

I'd read about grids in the Paranormal Friends Society newsletter, but I had never experienced one firsthand. Grids were more likely to be found on the east coast, where the ground doesn't move as much. Hard to keep things aligned in an earthquake zone.

To get a better look at the space, I took a step back. My steel-toed boots tapped the tiles, echoing in the silence. I clapped, listening to the sound reverberate between the walls. For a second, I had the overwhelming urge to yodel, but I wasn't getting paid to play.

My trusty tackle box held a laser aligner. I retrieved it and pointed the red beam toward the far wall. It was straight. I walked to the first set of doors and pressed the aligner again. Another straight line formed. I put the aligner on the floor and checked again. Three for three. Not good.

Between the doors and the checkered floor, the Changs had accidentally created a grid. Shades loved grids. It was the equivalent of catnip to a cat or counting to an OCD vampire. The invisible lines gave Shades the power to partially manifest. This matched what the Changs had told me on the phone about the shadow men and levitating furniture.

Grids also created supernatural portals, which increased a Shade's strength and made them deadly—especially if the grid matched an electromagnetic field emanating from the ground.

My gut was telling me this one did. And my gut never lied.

No wonder this thing could rearrange the furniture. It was tapped into the ghostly equivalent of a power station. The Changs were lucky that it hadn't decided to move the house off its foundation. It probably would, given more time.

I whipped out my TriField EM meter and started a slow sweep of the room. The electromagnetic readings were normal at first, bouncing between low to moderate. When I reached the center of the foyer, the gauge hiccupped. By the time I'd made a full circle, the needle was buried in the red zone and the readings were off the chart.

The Changs had designed their home to be esthetically pleasing. And it was, if pleasing was defined as a giant revolving door for the dead.

There was no telling what had found its way to the portal and come through. This place could be a giant Shade hotel by now. I didn't like the idea that I could be dealing with multiple entities. It was hard enough to rid a property of one by driving them out of the house before they had a chance to leave on their own. I wasn't sure I could dispatch several.

What would that power feel like? How long would the rush last? I knew I was getting ahead of myself. I'd have to live through the eviction first.

Without thought, I stepped back until my shoulders hit the front door. My present position wouldn't help me if something nasty wanted to take a pound of my flesh, but like a child's security blanket, it made me feel better.

If I hadn't made it a policy to work alone, I'd be tempted to pull out my cell-phone and call in reinforcements from the local ghost hunter group. On second thought, the Paranormal Friends Society would be more of a hindrance than help.

They were Shade lovers, every last one of them, with mottos like "Free the ghosts, they were once people too," and my personal favorite, "Have you hugged your ghost today." I tried to tell them they weren't dealing with fucking

Casper, but they didn't want to hear it.

The level of stupidity never ceased to amaze me. How could you hug something that wouldn't think twice about snapping your loved one's neck?

My parent's horror-struck faces flashed in my mind. I closed my eyes as a wave of nausea hit and willed the image away. I couldn't think about them now. It was a distraction that would only piss me off. Or worse yet—get me killed.

The scented air changed, crackling as the energy began to build. Whatever was trying to come through was big. Real big. And powerful. With my luck, it would be nasty as all hell. Thank goodness Shades can't fully solidify. Catching a shadowy half-formed version would be bad enough.

The thought had barely left my mind, when the hair on my nape stood on end.

The lights on my EM meter lit up like a Christmas tree during a power surge. I shoved it in my pocket and reached into my tackle box for the electronic scrambler, or ES for short. It was created to disrupt a Shade's molecular structure. Like the electromagnetic pulse device that I designed myself—thanks to an online electronics course. The ES wasn't exactly street legal, but it was the best weapon to use until I found the source of the haunt. After that, it would be up to the pop divas to dispatch the entity.

Personally, I don't have a problem with pop music, but for some reason it annoys the hell out of Shades.

I turned the scrambler on. The aim of the ES was to get the Shade's attention. Much like a poke in the shoulder or a punch in the face. It wasn't as effective as the EMP, but I didn't want to short out the Changs' televisions, computers, and stereos, if I could avoid it. I wouldn't have to worry about damage to my equipment, since it had been covered with sheet steel in order to protect the circuits.

I pressed the button on the ES device, sending out a signal. It rolled through the home unhindered by walls and floors. It was too weak to travel far. If the Shade was still just gathering power, that little scrambler wave of energy would hurt like a real mother.

The response was immediate. The walls began to shake, sending pictures and paintings crashing to the floor. I winced when a thick frame cracked as it hit the tile. Hope that wasn't a real Monet.

A loud screech scored the air. I recoiled, which was hard to do when your back was already against a door. The sound grew in volume before morphing into a howl of anger. The air reeked of sour milk, gagging me.

Bangs and flopping noises came from door number one on the left. Cocking my head, I listened as something writhed in agony.

Looked like I had a winner.

About the Author

T.R. Allardice writes young adult, new adult, and humorous horror. She's a member of The Horror Writer's Association, International Thriller Writers, the Author's Guild, and Novelist Inc.

Connect with her online:
Twitter: www.twitter.com/trallardice
Facebook: http://www.facebook.com/trallardice
Website: http://www.trallardice.com

Join the T.R. Allardice Newsletter for upcoming releases, exclusive excerpts, cover reveals, random giveaways, travel photos and tips.